The Colorado Kid

Ben Baker was the most powerful man in the remote Montana settlement of Silver springs, but, even surrounded by a small army of hired guns, he was afraid. For Baker had many enemies and Brewster Doyle was one of the biggest.

Learning that Doyle has sent the infamous gunfighter Frank McCready to kill him, Baker decides to have his men bushwhack the next rider into town. After all, he might not know what McCready looks like but he knows there is only one trail into Silver Springs.

But the next rider to appear is the tall drifter known as the Colorado Kid. Fighting for his life in a battle not of his making, can he survive as Silver Springs is bathed in blood?

The Colorado Kid

Dale Mike Rogers

A Black Horse Western

ROBERT HALE · LONDON

© Dale Mike Rogers 2005
First published in Great Britain 2005

ISBN 0 7090 7635 5

Robert Hale Limited
Clerkenwell House
Clerkenwell Green
London EC1R 0HT

Typeset by
Derek Doyle & Associates, Shaw Heath.
Printed and bound in Great Britain by
Antony Rowe Limited, Wiltshire

*Dedicated to two lovely ladies, Jackie Autry
and Ruth Gordon*

ONE

Lightning forked down from the heavens far off in the distance as thunder rumbled all around the handsome grey mount. There was a chill in the air but the six-feet-six-inch-tall horseman astride his mount did not appear to notice. For he was from a place where the extremes of climate had toughened his soul and spirit long before he had reached this place. The sun raced across the shallow stream as if vainly attempting to defy the gathering storm clouds.

The lone rider drew back on his reins and stopped the tall mare.

His keen blue eyes darted around from beneath the wide brim of his Stetson and studied the unfamiliar terrain. Keeping the long Winchester gripped firmly in his right hand, he slowly dismounted in one well-practised flowing movement. There was a nervousness about the tall rider which kept his wits honed like a straight razor. The dried bloodstain on his sleeve and the crude repair to the fringed buckskin shirt showed that he had a right to be wary of any new place that he ventured into. For the bullets of unseen enemies had sought and found him many times before.

He loosened his grip on the reins and allowed the mare to drop her head and start drinking.

Yet he himself did not drink.

He continued to stand guard over the handsome animal as he continued to survey the trees and bushes which ran along the horizon ahead of him. His every instinct told him that there was someone or something out there. For he had been raised by people who had once lived unchallenged all over this land. A people who now numbered fewer than the buffalo.

His blue eyes looked up at the troubled sky. He could see the black clouds were gathering together as if they required union before they could unleash their fury. There were no birds to be seen or heard anywhere near the fast-flowing stream.

That concerned the giant man and he cradled his rifle in the crook of his arm. There should be birds, he thought. A lot of them near this place, and yet there were none at all.

Something had frightened them away from

the countless insects that danced over the top of the water in the last defiant rays of the sun.

He knew that it was not he who had done so. He could walk within feet of most birds without disturbing them. They did not fear him for they knew that he would not harm them.

Neither was it the approaching storm.

It had been something else which had caused them to flee this rich source of food.

The crystal-clear water stretched for more than twenty yards until it reached the six-foot-high swaying grass. An army could be concealed out there and no one would ever suspect, he thought.

No one but him.

He still had the instincts that he had learned in the high country from the Sioux; survival instincts which had been taught to him by the people who were now nearly extinct.

It was as if he could actually sense the danger he knew lay out there ahead of him.

He removed his water-bag from the saddle horn and removed its wooden stopper with his teeth. He held on to the rawhide strips which girdled the bag and lowered it into the stream. He remained upright and alert as the stream slowly filled the three-gallon capacity of the Indian water-container.

For more than ten years since he had emerged

from the wilderness as a youth, the tall horseman had drifted hundreds of miles north of his birthplace. Yet he could still not understand how a people who had lived in the lush forests since time itself had begun, could simply vanish.

But he had left them before the gold had been discovered and the white men had tried to buy their land from them. Before the battles and the ultimate destruction of practically an entire race had occurred.

Never having read any of the newspaper reports about Custer's last stand at the Little Bighorn or the vengeance of the cavalry, he had no way of knowing that the reason the forests had emptied was because most of the Sioux were dead.

He moved his moccasins and looked upstream and then down. It was as if he was searching for clues as to who it was whom he knew lay in wait across the stream.

There were no clues.

Few people who had encountered the quiet giant during the years that he had roamed the West ever forgot him. For he was unlike all other men. His sheer height and build made it impossible for anyone ever to allow his image to drift far from their thoughts. But it was also the fact that he was unique. Not quite a white man and yet not an Indian either. A man who saw both sides of the coin. Slow to temper and yet faster than most to react when attacked.

But no one knew his real name.

It was said that he had no real name.

Or that he had forgotten what it was after being raised by the Sioux.

The only thing that those who had met him agreed upon was that he was known as the Colorado Kid.

A strange name which was neither accurate nor descriptive, for he had never been anywhere near the territory called Colorado, nor was he the sort of man who could be thought of as ever being young enough to be described as a kid.

He seemed to be carved from granite.

Every inch of his awesome stature demanded respect. For he looked as if he were capable of tearing trees out of the ground with his bare hands.

The Colorado Kid was the size of a grizzly bear and yet no sculptor could have created a more perfect physique. There was not an ounce of spare fat on his entire being. Shoulders were solid muscle and a trim waist made it hard to imagine that this man had once lived with the far smaller Indians of the Great Basin. The only hint of his past was his straight black hair which was well-groomed, yet slightly longer than most white men wore it.

How he had come to be raised by the noble tribesmen of the vast forests, no one knew. Not even Colorado himself. Yet he was one of them.

A blood-brother to the people. That was what the many tribes of the Sioux nation called themselves. They were the people. Their father was the Great Spirit of the sky and their mother the earth itself.

Colorado accepted the nickname that the white men had given him for he knew that they would never be able to pronounce his Sioux name. If he had ever had a name before being adopted by the people who raised him as one of their own, he did not know it.

The six-feet-six-inch-tall horseman accepted that he would always be the Colorado Kid. Until, that was, he returned to the forests far to the north.

Until he found one of his people again.

He pulled the water-bag out of the cold water and returned the wooden stopper back to the neck of the leather container. He hung it on to the saddle horn and then stepped into the stream and narrowed his eyes.

There was definitely something a mile or so ahead.

He had caught subtle hints of its aroma on the morning air in his flared nostrils, but still could not tell what it was or see anything.

As the mare raised its head from the stream, Colorado stroked its neck, grabbed its flowing mane and then swiftly threw himself on to the saddle without using the stirrup. He gathered up the reins and urged the horse across the shallow water.

Lightning continued to trace across the blackening sky as the sun disappeared behind the storm clouds. A deafening explosion of sound erupted above the rider but neither the Kid or the horse flinched.

It took more than that to deter them.

The grey strode confidently through the stream as its master continued to study everything around him. The cool water lapped over the hoofs of the animal, washing away a score of miles of trail dust.

Whatever it was that had caused his senses to alert him to the possibility of danger, the Colorado Kid was determined to find it before it found him.

The mare started to gather pace as it raced through the stream and into the tall swaying grass on the riverbank.

TWO

For more than three miles Colorado had aimed his tall mount deeper and deeper into the uncharted land. The storm was growing more and more violent with every step that his obedient horse took through the softening ground. The vicious rain lashed down and cut into the rider and mare like the whips of a million unseen enemies.

Yet Colorado still saw nothing except the mocking rain as he steered his mount through the tall swaying grass. The expert horseman knew that the danger was still out there, waiting like a coiled rattler ready to strike. For a decade he had ridden into one bushwhacking after another as he roamed the West that the law had yet to discover.

For a while he had wondered why there were so many men who lived by killing and stealing.

Then he had realized that these were not real men at all, but mere animals in human form. Scum who craved anything that others had. They would kill to steal the beef jerky in a stranger's saddle-bags. The temptation of laying their hands on a horse and its tack was irresistible to their breed. Add the guns and ammunition to the pot and it was amazing that anyone ever managed to get from one remote town to another without being either wounded or killed.

Colorado had worked hard to obtain his meagre possessions and was not going to give them up without a fight. The scars on his body were proof of that.

Lightning lit up the heavens again.

The Kid teased the reins back in his large hands and then sat motionless astride the obedient mount. The deafening storm was now directly overhead and he could feel the driving rain on his chiselled features as it cut through the cold air.

It was hard for the horseman to believe that it was still only half-way through the morning. The rays of the sun had been completely blotted out. It had grown increasingly dark as the black thunderclouds swirled around in the heavens above him. The deadly forks of lightning grew more and more frequent as they cut down and struck at the ground all around him.

Yet neither Colorado or his bedraggled horse flinched.

Even as the storm reached its height, his well-trained grey mare remained perfectly still as its master stood, balanced in his stirrups and surveyed the surrounding land from his high vantage point.

Suddenly, his eyes focused on something metallic a quarter of a mile ahead of him as sheet lightning flashed and illuminated the sea of tall moving grass for a few seconds.

It was only a brief glimpse but enough to confirm Colorado's suspicions.

Slowly he lowered himself on to his saddle and wrapped the reins around his left wrist. He knew that whoever it was out there, he had a Winchester.

The question was: was the rifleman waiting for him? Or was there other prey in this quagmire?

The Colorado Kid slapped the loose ends of his reins across the mare's shoulders and urged it to continue walking. The horse responded immediately.

As the mare climbed higher ground he wondered how close the sniper was. Then, as another twisted fork of lethal lightning cut down from the brooding black clouds and hit the ground a mere hundred yards from his mount, Colorado heard something to his left.

It was an unmistakable sound that he recognized.

It was the hammer of a Winchester being pulled back until it locked fully into position.

There was no time to lose, he thought.

All Colorado's questions had been answered.

The rifleman was not waiting to try and kill himself a meal, he was waiting to kill him. The Kid shook his reins free of his wrist, removed his feet from the stirrups and then rolled off his high saddle.

His feet hit the muddy ground as the sound of the bullet being fired filled the cold air.

His narrowed eyes saw its red-hot trail speed over the neck of the grey.

Too close! Colorado grabbed the reins and used every ounce of his incredible strength to drag the horse down until it was on its knees beside him. Colorado kept pulling until the horse was lying on its side. Resting on one knee, he ran a hand over the mare's face and then released his grip on the long leather reins.

'Stay there, girl!' he commanded the wide-eyed beast. As always, the horse obeyed its master.

He pulled his Peacemaker from its long holster and cocked its hammer as another shot rang out. His screwed-up eyes saw the tips of the grass disintegrate above him as the second rifle bullet searched vainly for its target.

Colorado looked all around him as if he were trying to find another way to get to the man who was intent on claiming his life.

But there was only one choice.

One way to attack an attacker, and that was head on.

The Kid leapt over the belly of the horse and ran through the driving rain and swaying grass straight toward the place from where he knew the rifle had been fired.

A third and fourth shot blasted out from the barrel of the rifle, sending its bullets over the head of the fast-moving Kid, who refused to slow his pace through the sodden ground.

He continued running until his keen instincts spotted the patch of dry grass. He stopped and knelt beside the place where he knew the sniper had tried to claim his life.

Colorado ran the palm of his left hand over the dry grass as his ears and eyes sought out the mysterious rifleman. He gripped his handgun firmly and then spotted the footprint depressions on the crushed-down grass.

The rifleman had moved away quickly, he thought.

The tall figure rose up to his full height and stared off into the half-light.

'You can run but you cannot hide!' he

muttered under his breath. Then he started to follow the trail.

Even the blinding rain that mercilessly stung his eyes could not deter him.

Colorado was no longer the hunted.

He was now the hunter!

THREE

The ground seemed to slide away from beneath Colorado's moccasins as he forced his way through the driving rain and high brush to which the swaying grass was now giving way. The rifleman who had fled when he realized that the tables had been turned on him had left a clear trail to the trained eye.

Colorado stalked his way after the bush-whacker like a bloodhound on the trail of a raccoon. He paused and knelt on the wet uneven ground for a few seconds and listened.

The aroma of the sniper's mount hung on the cold air and had grown stronger in his flared nostrils the further down the slope he had travelled. The Kid knew that his prey was heading for his horse.

Colorado turned his head, cupped his left hand to his face and whistled. He then returned his attention to the broken brush ahead of him and rested the long-barrelled gun on his knee.

He could hear his grey mare following behind him as his whistle had instructed. It would take the tall animal at least five minutes to reach its master.

Then Colorado noticed that the rain had ceased.

He removed his hat and shook it as a shaft of sunlight managed to penetrate the black clouds.

It was as if some heavenly body was pointing to a place far below him. The tall man slowly rose to his full height and placed his hat over his well groomed black hair. His blue eyes trailed the light from the sky down to the ground.

Then he saw the flashing of gun metal again.

Colorado was about to move when he saw a plume of smoke and heard the crack of rifle fire. The bullet tore the Stetson from his head before the Kid had time to react.

He felt the warmth of blood trickling down from the top of his head and over his brow and face.

'Big mistake, stranger!' Colorado said as he fanned the hammer of his gun.

Three bullets cut their way through the brush and down the slope. Three deadly accurate bullets.

Colorado knew that the rifleman was dead

before he slid his gun back into the holster and turned to see his mount coming through the undergrowth towards him.

The mare walked to his side and stopped.

Colorado held the flowing grey mane and threw himself on to the saddle. He leaned back and allowed the horse to walk down the slippery slope at its own pace.

'Easy, girl!' the Kid said as they found the crumpled figure lying beside his still-smoking rifle.

The mare stopped.

Colorado dismounted, pulled the dead man over and looked at the expressionless face. A trickle of blood seeped from the corner of the corpse's mouth.

Colorado shook his head, then straightened up.

Whoever this back-shooter was, he was unknown to the Kid.

His eyes searched for the horse that he knew was somewhere close. Then he saw it. Its reins were tied firmly to a stout tree branch.

Colorado stepped over the body and made his way over the wet ground to the skittish horse. He pulled a long-bladed knife from his belt and sliced through the reins. The horse shied away from the tall man, then galloped off into the dense brush.

The Kid turned and glanced at his own mount before he returned to the body. He knelt down and pulled open the blood-soaked top coat. His three bullets had left a neat pattern on the filthy shirt.

Colorado carefully pulled out a wallet from the inside pocket and opened it. There was nothing in it except a well-worn business card with faded printing on one side.

He read it aloud.

BEN BAKER, ATTORNEY AT LAW, CRUCIBLE BUILD-ING, MAIN STREET, SILVER SPRINGS, MONTANA,

Colorado slid the card into one of his breast pockets thoughtfully. It was quite obvious that this dead man was not an attorney. So why did this creature have the card?

And who was Ben Baker?

He stood back up and then returned to his horse. He threw himself on top of the mount and steadied himself.

The sun was warm as it spread its rays across the wet land that surrounded him.

He felt the blood trickle down from the graze on his head and watched it drip on to the saddle horn. He touched it and then glanced at the body again.

'Why?' Colorado whispered. 'Why'd you want to try and bushwhack me?'

FOUR

Silver Springs was nestled in a fertile valley surrounded by high ore-rich hills and mountains. It had grown from a city of tents a mere five years earlier, to become a prosperous settlement of more than a hundred buildings. Montana could boast few similar towns within its boundaries; it had become better-known for its lush grazing pastures to the east, which had drawn cattle ranchers from less hospitable terrains.

Yet Silver Springs seemed to be almost hiding in the scenic valley between the mountains. A place where outsiders were not welcome and those who did manage to penetrate its defences knew that it was wiser to continue on their journey as quickly as possible.

The weekly stagecoach that trailed its way in and out of the valley seldom brought anyone except men in well-tailored suits with fat wallets and an eye for top-grade silver ore.

It was clear, though, that this was a place where wealth had chosen to spoil the people who resided in its opulent array of buildings.

The Colorado Kid might never have known it even existed at all if it had not been for the smoke that snaked up into the skies from the scores of blackened chimneys that topped its buildings.

Smoke that had the aroma of wood which had never quite managed to dry out in the damp valley.

He had spotted it after guiding his horse up to the highest point on a tree-covered mountainside after leaving the dead body of the bushwhacker far behind him. His tracking skills had come in useful as he followed the broken brush left by his unknown attacker. The dead sniper had forged his way through almost virgin vegetation to get to the spot where he had waited to kill the Kid.

It had been a simple task for Colorado to retrace the route back to Silver Springs.

The tall horseman drew back on his reins and studied the spot far below him. It was a valley far greener than any he had ever encountered before. But with an abundance of well-nourished trees and brush always came a dampness in the air. A dampness that could gnaw its way into a man's bones.

Colorado knew that this was a climate that could cripple even the strongest of souls given enough time.

He also knew that only well-fed stoves and fire-places could keep that dampness at bay. Colorado studied all the chimney-stacks and the black smoke that trailed up from them. As he inhaled the scent of the smoke he recalled his youth and the fires that the Sioux used to warm their bodies and souls. He noted that at least half the buildings had their fires lit.

They must be feeling cold, he thought.

Yet Colorado still felt nothing except the warmth of the sun on his back as it bathed the side of the mountain trail with its glorious after-noon light.

He ran his fingers through his black hair. The wound had stopped bleeding but was still tender to the touch. He squinted and shielded his eyes, realizing that he had not retrieved his hat after it was shot off his head back near the stream.

It was hard to make out any detail in the town far below him due to the abundance of large trees in full leaf. But he knew that this had to be the 'Silver Springs' that was on the card he had taken from the dead man's wallet.

He could still not work out why the attorney's card had been carried by the hapless rifleman.

Had Ben Baker sent the man to ambush someone?

If so, who?

But who was Ben Baker?

The Kid glanced at the trodden-down ground and the snapped branches of the brush and trees beside him. This was where the back-shooter had ridden from earlier that same day. He could still see the hoof-prints on the muddy ground.

Again he tried to work out why the rifleman had chosen to try and kill him.

It still did not make any sense.

No one knew that the Kid was coming that way, and yet the man had been waiting there for hours. Colorado knew that the man had been there for hours because of the way the crushed-down grass where the sniper had been sitting had been bone-dry. He had remained there even after the heavens had opened up and the rain had come.

Colorado rubbed his chin.

The sniper must have mistaken him for someone else. But who did these people fear enough to try and execute them?

So many questions and not one answer.

Colorado pulled the card from his pocket and

looked at it again. Maybe Ben Baker had the answers he sought.

There was only one way to find out.

He returned the card to his pocket and then glanced at the rooftops again.

Silver Springs was a town that looked quiet enough but looks could be deceptive. He had learned that the hard way many, many times in the past.

He pulled his gun from its holster and opened its chamber, removed the spent cartridges and tossed them away. With his fingernails he drew out fresh bullets from his gunbelt and slid them into the empty chambers.

Colorado holstered the weapon, then tapped his heels against the sides of the grey.

'On, girl,' he said.

The tall grey mare obeyed and continued on along the trail left by the dead man hours earlier. It led around the side of the high mountain and started to descend slowly towards the town far below.

Colorado glanced to his left. It was an awfully long way down, he thought. Not a place for a rider who feared heights or had no faith in his mount's courage. But the Kid knew that it was not the fall that killed you, it was hitting the ground that did the damage.

With every stride of his horse's long legs

Colorado's keen eyes studied everything above and below the trail. He could hear noises somewhere ahead. He listened to strange sounds which he could not identify coming from further down the trail. Muffled noises that were unlike anything he had ever heard before.

Suddenly, to its master's surprise, the grey mare hesitated and pulled back. Colorado grabbed the horse's mane and steadied it. He then threw his right leg over the animal's neck and slid to the ground.

He landed silently and drew his Peacemaker. His thumb pulled its hammer back until it locked fully into position.

His blue eyes darted all around him as the mare lowered its head and stroked at the ground.

'What is it, girl?' Colorado whispered to the animal. 'What you seen?'

The horse shook its head as if in answer.

The Kid's eyes darted in the direction that his faithful mount was indicating. He narrowed his eyes and focused every instinct on the place a mere fifty feet below them on the winding trail.

At first it just looked like the rest of the bright-green trail scenery. Branches swayed in the gentle breeze. Then he saw something that drew his total attention.

A brief hint of a black shadow flickered

beyond the thick vegetation, close to the high wall of undergrowth. He could just make it out behind the abundant greenery. That was where the noise was coming from.

A cave!

It seemed strange to him that there would be any caves up here. But then he thought about the name on the card. Silver Springs indicated that there was either silver here or a spring, or both.

The Colorado Kid stepped in front of his mount and aimed the gun at hip-height at the place his entire being told him to be wary of.

Silently, he strode towards the curious black shadow ahead of him. It was a cave, he thought. But it was not a natural creation; it had been crudely carved out of the mountainside by the hands of men seeking its precious silver ore.

The closer he got, the larger it appeared.

Colorado stopped several yards away from the mouth of the cave and studied it carefully. Rusting railtracks came out of the tunnel's black depths and stopped just outside the mouth of the cave. A pile of rubble near the edge of the steep drop showed how the miners disposed of their wasted efforts. They simply dumped it into the overgrown green valley. Colorado wondered how much ore they extracted compared to the vast quantity of rock and earth.

The muffled noise was still coming from within the depths of the dark tunnel. It was the sound of shovels and pickaxes being employed to fill a railroad truck.

Colorado knew that the men working inside the cave might not take kindly to any strangers around their claim. He had no desire to encounter any short-tempered miners. He turned and waved to his horse. The mare walked down the muddy trail towards him and stopped at his side.

He holstered his gun, grabbed the horse's mane, threw himself into his saddle and gathered up his reins.

Just as he started towards the town in the valley, he heard something behind him as it emerged from the dense brush.

He heard the unmistakable sound of a scatter-gun's twin hammers being hastily engaged.

Before the Kid could turn, he heard the deafening blast of both barrels being fired. He felt the heat of shot as it went over his head.

The startled mare reared up.

Colorado felt himself falling backwards over the saddle cantle. He tried to grab his reins but they slipped through his fingers.

He hit the ground hard.

FIVE

Every sinew in his body hurt as he lay on the wet trail. It was a stunned and dazed Colorado who stared up at the afternoon sky as his head cleared. Then he noticed the rounded figure of the man with the scattergun looking down at him curiously.

The miner had a beard which covered most of his face and seemed to meet his limp long hair and eyebrows until only a red nose and a pair of watery eyes were visible.

The man cranked the scattergun apart and smoking hot cartridges were expelled from its barrels. Before Colorado had time to blink, the miner inserted two fresh shells and jerked the gun back together again.

'Make just one move, stranger,' the miner said. 'One move and it'll be your last!'

The Kid inhaled deeply as he heard two more

men running out from the cave-mouth. He tilted his head and watched them run to their friend's side.

'I'm not intending to move until you say that it's OK, partner!' Colorado sighed.

'Who is he, Buck?' one of the miners asked the man holding tightly on to the scattergun.

'Looks like a claim-jumper to me!' another said.

The miner with the scattergun aimed both barrels at the prostrate Colorado's head.

'Start talkin', boy!'

'They call me Colorado!'

The three miners looked at one another with exactly the same blank expression etched on their bewhiskered features. The gun barrel was pushed even closer towards the Kid's face. He could smell the gunsmoke and feel the heat from the hot metal.

'Say again?' Buck queried.

'Colorado. They call me Colorado.'

'He looks like an Injun to me,' said the oldest-looking miner, as he ran his dripping nose along his sleeve.

'There ain't never been an Injun that big, Seth!'

'Look at his clothes, Buck. That's Injun buck-skin.'

Buck Harper shook his head.

'If he's an Injun, where's his feathers?'

'Buck's right. He ain't got a single feather.' The third miner, called Jonah Schmit, nodded furiously until it looked as if his head might fall off. 'I never seen an Injun without no feathers sticking out of his hair.'

Seth Marsh pointed down at Colorado's face.

'And he's got blue eyes. Never seen an Injun with blue eyes either. This ain't no Injun.'

The miner with the hefty weapon in his hands rolled his own eyes and shook his head.

'Then what in tarnation is he?'

Colorado carefully raised his left hand from the muddy ground and signalled to his three captors.

'I ain't a claim-jumper. I was just making my way to that town below. That is Silver Springs, ain't it?'

'Yep. That's Silver Springs OK,' Jonah answered before his two partners could speak. 'And a real awful place it is. What you want to go there for, sonny?'

'A varmint tried to kill me earlier. I traced his trail back here,' Colorado replied.

'What happened to this varmint, sonny?'

The Kid gritted his teeth.

'I got the better of him.'

'Kill him?'

'Yep.'

The three men looked at each other again and nodded. They appeared to be impressed.

'You reckon this critter used this trail?' Buck Harper asked.

'Yep. This morning,' Colorado replied.

'That must have been Poke Lucas, boys. I seen the dirty guttersnipe riding past here at first light. So that's what he was up to.'

Seth Marsh smiled enough for his eyes to wrinkle up above his beard.

'I never liked Poke. I'm glad he's dead. Ain't you boys glad he's dead?'

The other two miners agreed.

'Can I get up, boys?' Colorado asked.

'Sure you can.' Buck laughed. 'You done good killing old Poke. Nobody liked the rat.'

Carefully, Colorado eased his back off the ground and slowly rose up until he was standing beside the silver-miners. The trio gasped as they watched him stretch his aching frame until it reached its full height.

'Damn!' Buck gulped. 'He ain't an Injun. He's a real livin', breathin' giant, boys!'

The three men circled the Kid as he checked himself for bruises. Their faces showed their total disbelief at the sheer size of the man they had managed to get the better of.

'Are you a real giant, son?' Jonah asked sheepishly.

Seth shook his head as he listened to his fellow-miner.

'Don't talk loco, Jonah. There ain't no such thing as a real giant. That's only in story-books.'

Jonah inched forward, touched the kid's arm, then backed off.

'He's real enough, Seth. We caught us a real blue-eyed giant!'

Buck Harper sighed heavily and looked hard up into the kid's well-honed features. The back of his neck hurt as he tried to focus on the man who appeared like a giant redwood compared to them.

'What did you say your name was, sonny?'

'Colorado. Some call me the Colorado Kid.'

Jonah chuckled and walked around the huge man as if he were inspecting every inch of Colorado's impressive frame.

'Biggest darn kid I ever done seen. I'd hate to see a grown-up from wherever it is that you hail from.'

'What you doin' here, Kid? If ya killed Poke, there ain't no call for you to stay here.'

'I'm just riding through. I ain't after your goods,' Colorado said. 'I ain't no thief. But I am retracing the trail of a bushwhacker. And that trail led right past your claim. I reckon that I could have just headed on my way after I got the better of that bushwhacker, but I figured he was

36

paid to kill someone. I wanted to find out who paid Poke Lucas and why.'

'I believe him, boys,' Jonah said. 'But curiosity killed the cat, sonny.'

The other two miners agreed. They'd seen their share of claim-jumpers over the years that they had toiled in the mountains. The Kid was no claim-jumper.

Colorado glanced over their heads and spotted his faithful mount standing less than ten feet behind them. He relaxed with relief to know that she had not been harmed.

'How come you reckon that Silver Springs ain't a very nice place to visit, boys?' the Kid asked in a low drawl.

' 'Coz it's full of vermin.' Seth spat. 'The human sort, if you get my drift.'

Colorado nodded.

'I reckon I do. What they do to make you boys dislike them so much?'

'They cheat on the price they pay us for our ore,' Jonah piped up quickly. 'They never pay more than fifty cents on the dollar of its true worth. They know that we ain't got time to go lookin' for other places to sell our goods. So they just cheat us and all the other miners in the hills.'

Colorado nodded again.

'Who was this Poke Lucas critter you mentioned?'

'We already told you. He was scum,' Buck replied, still clutching his scattergun firmly in his rough hands. 'A hired gun by all accounts. They reckon he killed for money.'

'Did he work for anyone in particular?' Colorado was getting even more confused the more he learned about the town below them and its citizens.

'Yep. A lawyer named Ben Baker,' Seth piped up. 'He weren't the only one, though. Baker has a string of the dirty rats on his pay-roll down there.'

Colorado rubbed his chin and walked to a large boulder. He rested his aching rump on it and studied the trio of silver-miners carefully. They were honest, hard-working men. That was obvious. He always trusted men who bore the scars of their labours on their hands.

'Why would a lawyer need hired guns?'

'Reckon he's protecting his money.' Jonah shrugged.

'How many men has Baker got?' asked the Kid with a sigh.

'Last time we was down there, we seen at least ten or more heavily armed critters hanging around Baker like flies round a dung heap.' Jonah spat.

'More like twenty!' Buck corrected.

Seth's head bobbed up and down. 'Twenty! Yep! Twenty!'

Colorado tapped his large fingers together.

'Is Baker the head honcho down there?'

The three men looked at one another. It was a good question and one that deserved an answer.

Buck stepped forward and rested his own backside on the boulder beside the huge figure. He smoothed his beard down away from his lower lip and glanced at the Kid.

'No he ain't. Leastways, he ain't 'sposed to be, Kid. Silver Springs got itself a mayor.'

'A mayor?' The Kid repeated the word.

'Yep! Old Jeb Carter. He's the mayor.' Buck looked at the faces of his two friends as if trying to get confirmation. 'Right, boys?'

Both Marsh and Schmit nodded.

'Does Carter have hired guns too?' the Kid asked.

'Not that we know of, Kid,' Buck replied for the three of them. 'Say, that is curious, ain't it?'

Colorado nodded.

'Darn curious, boys.'

SIX

The magnificent grey mare entered the outskirts of Silver Springs cautiously and walked slowly along the narrow streets with its ears pricked. Like its master, it knew that this was a dangerous place. The three miners far above on the high mountain trail had given Colorado a lot to think about. A lot to worry about. The tall rider watched everything that moved as the miners warnings continued to fill his thoughts.

Silver Springs did not look dangerous.

Yet something was definitely wrong. For this was unlike any other town that he had ever ridden into. There were but a few of its citizens walking around. Those who were suddenly scurried away like frightened rabbits as soon as they spotted the horse and rider.

Colorado thought that strange. For even though he was far taller than the average drifter, he had never seen people flee from the mere sight of him before.

The afternoon sun still had a few hours remaining before it would sink below the high tree-lines which dominated the valley, and yet Silver Springs was like a ghost town.

The trail down towards Silver Springs had given the Kid good cover on his approach to the first of the buildings that marked the edge of the well maintained settlement.

A thousand fleeting thoughts ran through his mind.

But the main one kept returning over and over again.

Was this a trap?

If so, why would they want to trap a total stranger? Had it anything to do with the dead man he had left miles behind him, or the lawyer who surrounded himself with hired gunmen?

Why?

The thought continued to gnaw at his innards as he tapped his moccasins against the side of the slender grey and teased the reins with the fingers of his large left hand.

Colorado kept the palm of his right hand resting on the gun grip of his holstered Colt Peacemaker as he coaxed the horse towards what he took to be the main street.

His blue eyes darted from one window to

another as he vainly sought out the town's elusive inhabitants.

A bead of sweat trickled down from his black hair and traced over one cheekbone until it found his square jawline. In all his days, he had never felt quite so alone.

He was worried.

If Ben Baker was as bad as the three miners had painted him, and employed as many gunmen as they had implied, he was riding into trouble.

Colorado still could not understand why a lone bushwhacker had been waiting out on the trail. Were these people expecting someone else?

Someone whom they thought required killing?

It was a thought that would not have time to develop further in the tired mind of the horseman.

As his mount turned a leafy corner and walked into a much wider street, the Colorado Kid realized that his concerns were fully justified.

Suddenly, a blinding series of flashes appeared to come from almost every direction before the deafening sound stopped his horse in its tracks.

The street was filled with the acrid stench of gunpowder as the vicious volley of rifle fire cut through the air all around the high rider.

Colorado felt the impact as two of the bullets ripped through the left sleeve of his fringed buckskin jacket and tore at his muscular flesh.

He had felt the unmistakable pain before.

As blood poured from his wounded arm he dragged his reins hard to his left and stood in his stirrups. He drove the mare as hard as he could back along the street down which he had just ridden.

The animal had only just found its pace when the Kid spotted more armed men appearing from the gardens of houses that he had thought empty only a few moments earlier.

Eight heavily armed men moved from both sides of the street.

Before any of them could fire, Colorado hauled his reins back and twisted the mare's neck around to its right. He whipped the creature's shoulders and charged towards the closest of the buildings.

The guns started to open up.

The grey leapt the white picket-fence and thundered down the narrow gap between two houses. With every stride of his mount's long legs Colorado could hear the shots ringing out behind him.

Splinters of wood showered over the rider as he forced his horse into the back yard of the building. He turned the animal again and tried to work out the safest route away from the gunmen he could hear racing after him.

Colorado allowed the horse to back up as he faced a seven-foot-tall side-fence separating the two rear yards.

'Now!' The Kid screamed as he slapped the horse's rump with his right hand.

The grey mare burst into full flight and galloped at the fencing. Within five strides the horse had created enough momentum to leap over the high obstacle.

A moment after the mare had landed, Colorado pulled the reins back again and stopped the powerful animal in her tracks. He stood in his stirrups and spun around as he heard the sound of his pursuers entering the yard from which he had just managed to escape.

'Where is he?' a voice called out.

'Where'd he go?' another shouted over the noise of the rest of the heavily armed men.

Colorado knew that there was only one way he could go and that was over the rear wall. But it was at least ten feet high and there was no way of knowing what lay beyond it. He spun the horse again trying to find another, less impossible route away from the gunmen.

Then he saw the barrels of the men's weapons as they struggled to get over the wooden fence.

'C'mon, girl!' he shouted into the ears of his confused mount. 'We gotta try and jump it! Now!'

He drove the mare straight down the cultivated garden as hard as he could. The animal continued to gain speed as its hoofs dragged it closer and closer to the high wooden wall.

The Kid balanced himself in his stirrups and leaned as far back as he dared with the reins in his hands. The mare approached the fence at full gallop and then rose up into the air.

The rider gritted his teeth and narrowed his eyes when he saw that his tired mount could not attain the height it sought to clear the fence.

The leading hoofs hit the wall of wood a mere twelve inches below the top of the line of planks. Colorado watched as they snapped under the full weight of the animal beneath him.

Rusted nails and splinters cascaded in every direction as the mare continued through the gap in the fence which it had created by its sheer force.

The grey landed in a sea of undergrowth between two massive trees.

Before the Kid had managed to sit down in his saddle he heard the shots of the gunmen ringing out behind him again as one by one they tried to locate their elusive target.

Branches all around the tall rider were severed from the trees which surrounded him as one deadly red-hot bullet after another burned into the undergrowth.

His blue eyes glanced at his blood-soaked sleeve before he returned his attention to what lay before him. He was in pain and suddenly aware that the wounds were worse that he had first thought.

A thousand branding-irons could not have inflicted more pain on the horseman.

Colorado leaned over the neck of his horse and tried to calm the creature as his mind desperately tried to work out how they could get away from the fast-approaching gunmen.

It had been said many times that when the Kid sat in his saddle, he became part of the horse beneath him. It was as if man and beast thought with one mind. There were no more words that the rider could say to encourage the grey mare.

Now she knew exactly what had to be done. She had to save the life of her wounded master.

He clung to the mare's neck as the gallant animal crashed into the almost impenetrable undergrowth beyond the shattered fences and thundered into the forest.

There was no way of knowing where they were headed as more shots cut past the broad-shouldered rider, but they were seeking only one place.

A place where their enemies' bullets could not find them.

SEVEN

Gunsmoke still drifted on the cool afternoon air as the pair of blinkered chestnut geldings between the traces were stopped in their tracks by the heavy reins that were in the hands of the lawyer. Ben Baker wrapped the long reins around the buckboard's brake-pole and then climbed down to the ground. He could hear his hired gunmen approaching from behind the line of buildings as he surveyed the scene. The gun-toting group headed sheepishly towards their stone-faced paymaster.

The emotionless lawyer stood watching them. There was failure etched into every one of their unshaven faces. An embarrassment that appeared at odds with their arsenal of deadly weaponry.

Their prey had somehow eluded capture.

Ben Baker kicked at the ground. It was his

only display of anger as the men reached the buckboard.

'Where's his miserable body?' Baker asked. 'I thought that you'd bring it to me.'

'Things didn't quite go to plan, Mr Baker,' one of the men muttered from behind the wide shoulders of his cohorts.

'I reckon I ain't going to like this, am I?' The lawyer struck a match and cupped its flame to the end of his long thin cigar. He inhaled deeply and studied their smoking weapons. 'So which one of you cowards is going to spit it out? Admit it, you let him slip through your fingers.'

'He got away, Mr Baker!' said his top gun, named Tom Jardine. He stared at the ground before sliding both his guns into their holsters. He rested a hand on the buckboard and shook his head. 'I still can't figure it. He just up and got away. We fired so many bullets at him that you couldn't see through the gunsmoke.'

'But how could he get away?' Baker asked, smoke drifting between his gritted teeth.

'What ya mean?' Jardine looked at the stern-faced man who seemed to be staring off into the ocean of swaying green beyond the line of houses. 'He just did, that's all.'

Baker turned his head, pulled the cigar from his mouth and tapped the ash on to the ground.

'There are eighteen of you. How could you all

miss him, Tom? How is that possible?'

Jardine looked at the faces of his fellow hired guns. Each of them diverted his eyes from Jardine's. None was willing to accept his part in the dramatic failure.

'He rode through old man Hooper's back fence and high-tailed it off into the forest.'

Baker shook his head in disbelief.

'He just rode through a fence and got away?'

'He was fast!' Jardine shrugged. 'It was like he was glued to that grey of his. I never seen anyone ride like that in my whole life. He got that horse to jump over fences that it just ain't possible to jump over, Mr Baker.'

'His horse was fast and could jump, huh?' A frustrated Ben Baker sighed. 'I guess that none of you thought about shooting the horse and then shooting him, did you?'

Jardine rolled his eyes and kicked the wheel of the buckboard with all his might.

'Damn! Why didn't I shoot the horse?'

'Maybe it's because you're stupid, Tom!' Baker said. 'Just like the rest of this rancid bunch.'

'We winged him, though!' Grover Pyle chipped in. Pyle was a short stocky man with a shaven head. 'I found the blood, Mr Baker. A whole lotta blood! Look!'

Baker stared down at the short man's blood-covered left palm and almost smiled.

'At least one of you hit your target. It's a shame the rest of you couldn't manage to do the same. Now we've got to find him and finish him off, boys.'

Each of the gunmen lowered their heads as Baker strode around the group of heavily armed men. He inhaled on his cigar as if its stinking tobacco-smoke could help him think.

'We could trail the critter!' Jardine suggested. 'He headed off in the direction of the waterfall. There ain't no way out of the valley. He's trapped.'

Baker looked up at the sky for a brief instant, then returned his eyes to his own pacing feet.

'It'll be dark in less than two hours.'

'We could use torches!' Chill Smith, a youthful-looking yet cold-blooded killer added.

'Even a wounded man can shoot at a target holding a torch, Chill.' Baker climbed back up on to the driver's seat of his buckboard and gathered up his reins thoughtfully. 'He'll keep until sun-up. Who knows, maybe the night might finish him off for us.'

'I never seen anyone who could handle a horse like that varmint, Mr Baker,' Jardine said once more. 'He rode like an Injun.'

'He ain't no Indian, Tom. Frank McCready is many things, but he ain't an Indian.' Baker placed the cigar between his thin lips again and filled his lungs with the strong smoke. 'Reckon he won't get far if he's bleeding that badly. Plenty of time for us to track him down after we get ourselves a good night's sleep.'

Jardine stepped to below the driver seat and looked up at the lawyer's face. As always, it showed little emotion as Baker chewed on the end of the cigar.

'Who is this varmint, Mr Baker? Who is Frank McCready?'

Ben Baker glanced down. His eyes blazed.

'We set out after him tomorrow at dawn!'

'But who is he?' Jardine repeated. 'You sent Poke to bushwhack him but he still showed up in Silver Springs. Who the hell is this man? How come you want him dead so bad?'

'Dawn!' Baker growled. He slapped the heavy reins down on the backs of his matched pair of chestnut geldings. 'Meet me at dawn outside the Lucky Horseshoe or none of you gets paid this month.'

The eighteen men stepped back and watched the buckboard turn around in the street before it sped down towards the heart of Silver Springs.

Tom Jardine spat at the ground and looked at the men around him.

'Whoever McCready is, he sure has Ben spooked!'

'Yep. I never seen him so darned set on killing a critter before,' Grover Pyle agreed.

'But why?' Jardine muttered.

EIGHT

The moon was large and nearly orange. Countless stars sparkled in the almost cloudless sky above the rider as he forced his horse through the high, swaying grass. The tall black stallion began to shy as its master gripped his reins firmly. No amount of jagged encouragement from his sharp spurs could force the creature to take one more step in the direction that its master ruthlessly urged.

At last the muscular mount stopped completely, lowered its head and snorted angrily. It dragged a hoof over the muddy ground and then backed up by more than five feet.

The rider dismounted and dropped his reins to the ground. He hauled both his guns from his holsters and cocked their hammers before cautiously striding through the high grass.

Frank McCready was every inch the

gunfighter. The epitome of a deadly assassin. Nearly six feet in height and lean, clad now entirely in black leather. He had killed more than twenty men in his thirty years of existence. Most of them had required killing, but not all. Some were just the innocent victims who had strayed in front of the deadly barrels of his Colts. Men and women who had been marked for execution by someone willing to pay McCready's price.

For Frank McCready sold his services to anyone who was willing and able to pay his fee. To the gunfighter, it was nothing more than a job.

A career at which he excelled.

He cared nothing for his victims. Innocent or guilty, it made no difference. As long as he was paid his blood-money, he would fulfil his agreement. Never asking why. Never curious to know who his victims were. All he wanted was the money and he made sure that he got every cent.

McCready used the barrel of one his Colts to part the swaying grass. He stared down into the gully. The bright moon overhead illuminated the twisted dead body of Poke Lucas as it lay where it had fallen.

The bullet holes could be clearly seen amid the dried blood on the front of the gunman's shirt.

McCready strode down into the gully and then knelt. He released the hammers of his guns and then twirled them until they spun into his holsters. It was a trick that he had mastered long before he had chosen to hire his lethal skill out to the highest bidders.

His hands searched the body expertly, as they had done so many times before with the victims that he had slain during his lucrative if gory career.

McCready stood up and then spotted Lucas's Winchester a few yards away. He walked, plucked it off the ground and checked its magazine. It only had three bullets remaining in it. He sniffed the end of the barrel and could tell that it had been fired within the previous few hours. He tossed the rifle away angrily.

'Amateur!' he hissed.

Whoever this dead man was, McCready knew that he had probably been waiting to ambush him. He looked all around the area and then spotted the hoof-tracks left by the Colorado Kid's mount.

'I wonder who you are, mister. You sure can group your bullets together darn neatly,' McCready acknowledged. 'You killed this critter pretty good, but I wouldn't have needed three bullets. One would have done just fine.'

The gunfighter made his way back to his black

stallion. He grabbed his reins, stepped into his stirrup and hoisted himself atop the animal.

It was obvious to McCready that the dead bushwhacker had made a big error. He had mistaken the unknown rider for McCready himself. The gunfighter wondered who it was that had headed into Silver Springs ahead of him. Whoever he was, he might just regret visiting the town. For Ben Baker had been warned that someone was coming to kill him.

McCready laughed.

He then turned the head of the powerful horse and gave the body a wide berth. He jabbed his spurs hard into the flesh of the animal and continued his journey on towards Silver Springs.

As his mount gathered pace, the gunfighter kept wondering who had betrayed him. Who back in Dakota had wired Ben Baker that a hired killer was heading to Silver Springs to kill him? When McCready had left the cattle town of Twin Forks with $1,000 in gold coin in his saddle-bags he had not even considered that he might be riding into a trap.

Yet it was starting to look as if that was exactly what he was doing. Riding into a trap. He had accepted his fee and instructions from the wealthy Dakota cattleman, Brewster Doyle without question.

Doyle had many rivals and even more

enemies, any one of whom would do anything to see a hired killer turn on the powerful rancher.

McCready had ridden 150 miles along the Missouri River to this place without even considering that Doyle's rivals might have decided to warn Ben Baker.

That had to be it, he thought.

The more McCready thought about the man who had hired him, and the others who would do anything to try and bring down the most successful rancher in Dakota, the more he became convinced that he was right.

McCready knew nothing about Baker except that Doyle wanted him dead for some unknown reason. Yet that was how he always worked. He simply had the name of his victim and then did his best to kill them. Yet he knew nothing about Brewster Doyle either.

The cattle barons were a law unto themselves. They were always trying to destroy their enemies and then absorb their herds and thousands of acres of grazing land into their own already swollen empires.

They were men who never seemed to have enough.

They always wanted more. More money. More cattle and more land. McCready had worked for many such greedy creatures and yet this was the first time that it seemed that he might have been betrayed.

But it made little sense.

Spurring the stallion again and again, he began to realize that he was probably nothing more than a pawn in a deadly game of chess played by these wealthy cattlemen.

Yet that did not matter to him.

Perhaps Brewster Doyle's rivals hoped that the legendary Frank McCready might think that it was Doyle himself who had tried to send him to his death. Hoped that the gunfighter might decide to return to Twin Forks and seek vengeance on the man who had sent him on a fool's errand.

He drove the stallion harder and harder across the moonlit terrain. A million thoughts filled his usually coldly calculating mind. Perhaps he was simply imagining it all. Maybe the dead man far behind him had simply been the victim of a robber? Or the dead man might have been trying to rob another who was far better with his guns than he was with his Winchester. Could that be it, he wondered?

If any of Brewster Doyle's rivals had thought that Frank McCready was capable of seeking revenge, they were wrong. Not because there was any fear in the intrepid gunfighter, there was not. He feared no man and had never once even considered that he would ever meet anyone who might be a match for him when it came to a showdown. It was simply that he had no emotion at all in his entire being. He had never felt happiness, sadness or anything else which normal men feel.

Even curiosity was a rarity and something which never lasted long enough for him to understand.

Whatever the reality of his present situation, he continued to forge ahead atop the powerful black stallion.

For McCready was a professional.

In his three decades of life, he had never once lost his temper and only killed when he was paid to do so. Revenge was an emotion which was unknown to him. Something that he had yet to feel. To him, killing was simply a business he was employed to do. A profession that he was expert in.

Whatever the truth, McCready would do his utmost to earn his fee. He would execute Ben Baker and then decide what his next move would be.

After all, there was no profit in killing anyone for free.

NINE

It was as if the heavens were exploding in a crescendo of deafening sound. A million war drums could not have equalled the noise which filled the ears of the horse and rider as they approached. The waterfall towered fifty feet above the floor of the valley of dense under-growth and trees. The moonlight gave the never-ending white-water vapour a strange glow which drew the grey mare towards it like a moth to a naked flame.

The forested valley had given sanctuary to the injured horseman as his faithful mount had negotiated its entire length since fleeing the guns of Ben Baker's henchmen. Colorado had grown weaker and weaker with every mile that his grey mare had travelled.

The blood-soaked rider had almost lost his battle with consciousness the closer he got to the waterfall. Only the cool forest air which was filled with a million sounds and scents had managed to keep the injured Colorado Kid in his saddle.

He recognized them from his youth, when he had lived in a different forest. That had been another time and place. Another world which he knew he would never find again.

The tall grey mare had walked through the ice-cold river for more than two hours. But her master had barely noticed the course they had taken. It was all he could do to remain atop the alert horse. Every ounce of his quickly dwindling strength was required to maintain his balance. Yet it was a battle he was losing.

He had started to sway as the mare found deeper crystal-clear water to wade through. At last the large hands released their grip on the reins as the Kid's head filled with a strange fog he could neither understand or fight.

Colorado rolled helplessly to his side and then toppled like a felled tree from the high saddle into the fast-flowing water.

The sound of the splash was muffled by the pounding of the waterfall.

The ice-cold water was like a stick of dynamite to the senses of the Kid. Suddenly his mind was blasted wide awake to the realization that he was helpless. His massive frame was being washed down river like an autumn leaf.

The Kid tried to push himself out of the cold water which he knew would soon drown him, yet there seemed to be little strength left in his huge physique. He opened his blue eyes and stared up through the water at the shimmering image of the moon far above him in the heavens as it briefly managed to penetrate the dense tree-canopy.

Then even that was gone.

Over and over the helpless Kid rolled beneath the strong current. Colorado desperately tried to grab hold of something to aid his escape from the watery grave, but there was nothing his large fingers could find to assist him.

No floating tree-roots. Nothing except the fast-flowing water which continually came over the top of the falls and swept relentlessly between the river-banks.

The harder he fought, the more Colorado felt himself being washed further downstream. For the first time, the Kid realized that his immense strength had deserted him.

He was helpless to do anything except stare through the water as he rolled over and over beneath its surface. He could feel the last of his breath escaping his lungs and watched the bubbles swirl all around him.

Was this the end?

Then, abruptly, something stopped him. Had he hit a submerged log or the lodge of a family of beavers? Colorado tried to think but the ice-cold water seemed to numb his every thought.

Then he felt hands gripping his buckskin shirt-collar and pulling him toward the embankment. As his head came out from beneath the river water he gasped and coughed.

Colorado sucked in the precious air like a starving man given a meal for the first time in weeks. He had never realized how good it tasted before.

He could feel that he was being dragged up on to the dry river-bank by small but powerful hands. The Kid felt his shoulders being dropped on to the grass as the hands released their grip. Colorado tried to focus his eyes but the moon could not penetrate the dense foliage of the tree branches far above him.

Only the water that flowed over the falls, a few hundred yards away, seemed to be bathed in the eerie moonlight. There was a stark blackness which overwhelmed everything else in the forest.

He was exhausted by the loss of blood and his futile fight with the far stronger river-current. He continued to breathe in the sweet-tasting air as he listened to the feet moving around him. The Kid inhaled deeply and summoned up his remaining strength.

At last he managed to speak.

'Thanks. W . . . who are you?' he spluttered.

There was no reply. He felt two knees touch his arm as his saviour knelt down beside him and started to inspect his wounded arm.

A sound drew his attention. The Colorado Kid watched the silhouette of his grey mare trot up to within a few yards of where he rested. He turned his head back to the figure beside him and squinted hard at the face of the person who was cutting through his sleeve with a razor-sharp Bowie knife.

Eventually, Colorado began to make out the face above his own. He gasped again. This time it was due to utter surprise.

She was beautiful.

TEN

Jeb Carter had been the mayor of Silver Springs since the first elections had been held amongst its strange population. As a man who had once been a tower of strength in other towns across the West, he had been an obvious choice for the job that no one else either wanted or was qualified for. In those early years, when most of the town was made up of tents filled with silver-miners dreaming of the fortune that would change their lives for ever, Carter had managed to unite them all. His fairness in dealing with disputes between the various people within the valley had become almost legendary.

Yet for the past five years he had become little more than a puppet. A mere figurehead. A man who knew that he had lost what little power he had once enjoyed. The truth was a bitter pill for the thin silver-haired Carter to swallow.

The arrival of the mysterious Ben Baker and his army of hired guns five years earlier had changed everything. It had been a slow-burning fuse which none of the town's elders, especially Carter himself, had noticed. By the time they did, it seemed too late to reverse what had already happened.

Carter had been given the best of Silver Springs's houses to live in as long as he remained away from his office within the Crucible Building.

Since the arrival of the lawyer, Ben Baker, the mayor had seen his personal wealth grow and grow. At first he simply ignored the way that Baker went about handling the town's business, but then it started to become obvious that all was not well within the boundaries of Silver Springs.

There was a fear in the remote town now.

A fear that had grown like a cancer until it strangled the people who once lived in peace at the head of the valley settlement.

Jeb Carter had thought about standing up to Baker many times during the previous few months. He had even considered calling for a vote to see whether they should try and exile the devious and deadly lawyer.

Baker had responded with veiled threats. Until now, they had been enough to keep Carter under control. For when a man has nearly a score of hired gunmen working for him, only a courageous soul or a fool argues.

With the sounds of the gun battle still ringing in his ears, Jeb Carter strapped on his gunbelt and placed his hat on his neatly trimmed white hair.

He adjusted his red lace tie, then opened the front door of his home and stepped out into the quiet street. Dozens of streetlamps illuminated the way to the heart of the small town but even they could not light up every shadow or fool even the dimmest of people that this was not the night.

Darkness loomed all around Silver Springs as Carter walked determinedly along the wooden boardwalks toward Main Street.

For the first time in the five years since Ben Baker had arrived in the mining town, Carter felt his courage returning. He knew that there were many people in the town who felt exactly the same way as he did. His problem was that those very people seemed to be unable even to step out of their homes on to the streets after sundown any longer.

Carter knew that he was alone.

The gunmen had knocked on every door earlier that day, telling people to remain indoors because there was someone coming to Silver Springs whom Ben Baker wanted dead. To ignore this warning was to risk being caught in the cross-fire or worse, be executed for disobedience.

Carter had listened to the hundreds of shots being fired at the unknown rider from the relative safety of his home. With each shot, he had grown more and more angry.

Not with Baker or his henchmen.

He was angry with himself.

Angry because it had taken a virtual execution for him to wake up to the reality of what his life had become. For five years he had kept his head buried in the sand and not said or done anything to even try and curb the powers which Ben Baker had amassed.

Now at least he was going to try.

He stepped down from the boardwalk and crossed the street towards the telegraph office. The light from within the office shone forth from the window. The wires that were strung atop high poles buzzed above his head as his well-polished boots found the opposite board-walk and stepped up on to it.

Mayor Carter could see the man inside the office reading a newspaper, his stockinged feet perched on his desk. Carter turned the door-handle and entered.

Dwight Frye seemed startled. Nobody ever came to his office after dark, unless sent by Baker.

'Damn! You scared me, Jeb,' he muttered in a

stuttering tone that filled the small telegraph office. 'Ain't seen you out after dark for a coon's age.'

Carter nodded.

'Pull down the shades, Dwight.'

The man obeyed. The room was warm from a small coal-stove in its corner. A bucket of black coal stood next to the hot cast-iron stove.

'What's wrong, Jeb?'

Carter rubbed his jaw with his thumbnail.

'Has Baker received any wires lately, Dwight?'

The question chilled the fearful man as he sat at his cluttered desk. He shuffled the papers before him nervously.

'You know I can't talk about Baker's business.'

With the confidence that the drawn window-blinds gave the mayor, Carter leaned on the back of Frye's chair and whispered into the hair-filled ear.

'You can and you will, Dwight.'

'Baker would kill me if he found out.'

'Do you want me to kill you instead?' Carter sounded serious.

What little colour there was in the thin features of the telegraph man disappeared as he stared into the barrel of the drawn gun that was aimed at his temple.

'Are you serious, Jeb?' Frye croaked.

'Yep. I'll kill you if you don't tell me what I

want to know,' Carter growled.

Dwight Frye raised an eyebrow and sniffed at the air between them.

'Hey, Jeb. You ain't been sucking on a whiskey-bottle, have you?'

'Not yet. That'll come later when I've done what I have to do,' Carter replied.

The telegraph man gulped.

'I don't like the sound of that. What you intending on doing, Jeb?'

Carter cocked the hammer of his weapon and pressed its cold steel against Frye's face.

'Gimme the copies of every one of Baker's messages! Now!'

The man's shaking hands pulled open a drawer at his side and lifted up a notebook. Copies of every one of the previous months' wires were neatly noted in order. Frye handed the book to the mayor.

'Here! But don't you tell nobody that it was me who give it to you. OK?'

Carter did not answer. He thumbed through the book looking at every message. Then as he flicked over the page, his eyes focused on the short, brief warning that Ben Baker had been sent from Twin Forks two weeks earlier.

'Got it!'

Frye turned in his swivel chair to face the nodding mayor.

'What is it?'

Carter turned the book and pointed at the message.

'Don't you ever read these messages as you're taking them down, Dwight?'

Frye shook his head.

'It don't pay to get curious when it's Baker's wires you're jotting down, Jeb. Besides, that don't say nothing special.'

Jeb Carter cleared his throat and read the message out aloud.

'Ben Baker, lawyer. Silver Springs. Frank McCready is coming to town. Sent by Brewster Doyle. Has a job to do. You are that job. Signed, a friend.'

Frye shrugged.

'So? That ain't nothing special.'

'It is if'n you've heard of McCready. Do you happen to know who this McCready critter is, Dwight?' Carter asked.

He returned the book to the frightened man who immediately replaced it in the desk drawer.

'Nope. Who is he?' Frye asked. He locked the drawer and slid the key into his vest pocket.

'A hired killer!' Carter replied.

The telegraph man started to sweat.

'Oh my Lord!'

The mayor walked to the window, pulled the window-blind away and stared out into the quiet street. He could see a line of horses tied up outside the saloon a hundred yards away from the small office. They were the horses of Baker's henchmen.

'So that's who Baker set his vermin on earlier.'

Frye felt sick.

'I don't wanna hear no more, Jeb. What in tarnation is going on? How come you are so darn interested anyway?'

Carter slid his gun back into his holster.

'Ben Baker has to be stopped, Dwight. He's run roughshod over this town for years now and I let him. But now I'm going to stop the bastard.'

Frye jumped out of his chair and grabbed the arms of the brooding man.

'Are you loco? To even think of going up against Baker is just darn suicidal, Jeb. That man has too many guns on his pay-roll. They'll kill anyone who tries to get the drop on Baker, for sure. Even you!'

Carter sighed.

'Yeah! There was a time when I could have handled most of them with this old Colt. But now, I'm not sure.'

Frye rubbed his dry mouth with his fingers and thumbs.

'I heard me a few whispers earlier. They reckon that Baker's men didn't kill that rider. He rode off into the valley. They say he's wounded but ain't dead.'

Carter eyed the smaller man.

'McCready's wounded?'

'That's the rumour, Jeb. He rode off towards the falls.'

Jeb Carter smiled.

'Do you reckon McCready would like someone to help him?'

'You ain't thinking of going after a deadly hired killer, are you?' Frye gasped.

The mayor did not answer as he opened the door and inhaled the cool night air. He stepped out and stared across at the saloon before turning towards the trembling man beside him.

'I'm going to the livery stable, Dwight. Got me an idea that my horse could use a little exercise.'

Frye watched the man step off the boardwalk and head in the direction of the livery stables. He closed the door and rested his back against its solid surface.

'Jeb must be loco!' he said to himself. 'I sure wish that I had half his grit, though.'

ELEVEN

The sound echoed all through the Crucible Building. It was a mixture of panic and uncontrollable excitement. A confusion of noise. Ben Baker heard the running footsteps as they raced up the bare boards of the stairs and headed towards his office. He lifted his gun off the ink-blotter and hauled its hammer back with his thumb. He aimed its six-inch barrel at the door and waited. The sound of the running footsteps grew louder and louder as they echoed off the walls of the corridor and approached.

On any other day, Baker might have realized that it was the youngest of his hired gunmen, Chill Smith. But this had been no normal day.

Baker felt himself hesitate even to breathe. Every ounce of his concentration was on the door with its smoked-glass window as the shadow grew larger and larger.

He raised his hand and tried to stop the heavy weapon from shaking in his sweating palm. It was virtually impossible.

Then the door came bursting open.

Without even thinking, Baker squeezed the trigger.

A deafening blast filled the entire building as the barrel of the gun spewed out the bullet.

Chill Smith dropped to his knees and stopped shouting as he checked himself for damage. Then, when he saw Baker lower the gun on top of the desk, the young gunman rose to his feet and gave a huge sigh of relief.

'Reckon I kinda spooked ya, Mr Baker. Huh?' he said.

Baker nodded silently.

The gunman saw the hole in the wall a few feet above the door and smiled to himself.

'I figure that's why you pay us to do ya shootin' for ya.'

'What do you want, Chill?' Baker growled.

'Tom saw old Jeb Carter light out on his horse,' Smith answered. He coyly approached the desk where the gun still lay smoking on top of the ink-blotter.

The simple statement made Baker sit up abruptly.

'Carter rode out? Where was he headed?'

'He went into the forest. Towards the falls.'

Baker rose to his feet, leaving his chair spinning round on its base.

'The way that McCready went?'

'Yep. The same, Mr Baker.' Smith nodded like a donkey.

'But why?' Ben Baker lifted a half-smoked cigar from a large glass ashtray and placed it between his teeth. 'What the hell does that old fool think he's doing? Don't he know that Frank McCready's in the forest?'

'Some folks say that he's gone lookin' for him.'

Baker struck a match and stared at its flame.

'What would he be going looking for McCready for, Chill?'

'Beats me.'

Baker touched the end of the cigar and inhaled.

'Unless he's gotten a plumb loco idea that he might be able to use McCready to get back his town.'

The henchman had no idea what his boss was mumbling about but continued to nod anyway. He watched as Baker grabbed his gun and tucked it into his belt. Then he walked to his hatstand and plucked the Stetson off its peg.

'What ya thinkin' of doing, Mr Baker?' Smith asked.

Baker strode out into the corridor with the

confused gunman on his heels. He made his way down the flight of steps. At the bottom he was faced with the door to Main Street. He hauled it open and only stopped when greeted by the cool evening air.

'Jeb Carter might just have found his backbone, Chill,' he muttered through the cigarsmoke.

His young companion panted like a tired hound beside him.

'Backbone?'

Baker rolled his eyes. He suddenly remembered that he did not hire any of his men for their intelligence.

'Carter might have started to get his guts back.'

'So?' Smith pulled up his collar against the cool breeze which was cutting its way through the long, wide thoroughfare.

'What if he meets up with McCready?'

'Is McCready dangerous?'

Ben Baker turned and looked at the face beside him. A face that could not hide the lack of imagination inside its skull.

'McCready was hired to come to Silver Springs to kill me, Chill,' he explained. 'Now do you understand?'

Smith nodded again.

'Now I understand.'

'Thank God!' Baker headed towards the saloon with his man a few paces behind him.

'Don't he like you?'

The lawyer did not reply. He increased his pace until he forced his way through the swing-doors of the saloon. He looked around for his men. He knew that even though he had told them to be waiting outside the drinking-hole at dawn, none of them would have even considered getting any sleep.

He spotted Tom Jardine first.

'Get the men together, Tom!' Baker shouted above the sound of a tinny piano. 'We're heading into the valley after McCready right now!'

Jardine finished his glass of whiskey and did exactly as instructed. There were no questions. Ben Baker had given an order and they were paid to obey.

TWELVE

The only sound within the small one-room cabin was that of the burning kindling as it crackled beneath the cast-iron stewpot set amid the flames. The Kid stared at the face of the beautiful young female as the firelight danced around the cabin's almost bare interior. He imagined that she had to be about twenty years of age but Colorado could not be certain. The tattered dress she wore seemed far too small for her, as if she had outgrown it long ago. He could tell that she had added bits to it over the years to try and fend off the damp forest climate, but what was left of the original garment still showed.

It was worn and ragged, and hardly a hint of its original colour remained, but it could still be made out by a keen well-trained eye.

This was no forest woman. This was someone who had been disowned by her own people and left to die in this forest, he thought.

Somehow, she had survived.

He glanced at his sleeve. The ice-cold river had washed most of the blood off it. She had sewn up his ripped flesh and the buckskin shirt-sleeve after bathing the wound with medicinal moss.

He had seen the Sioux use the same moss to heal cuts many times during his youth.

Colorado wondered how she knew of the healing properties of such things. How long had she been abandoned in this forest valley? She certainly was no Indian.

Again he thought of what her name might be. There were no clues to be seen within the four walls of the cabin. No hint of her identity.

Was she like him? With no real name at all?

She sat on a two-foot-high chopping-block watching him as he rested in the only soft chair. He cupped a bowl of aromatic broth in his large hands and sipped at it slowly. It was good and he could feel its purity warming his innards. It had been a long time since he had tasted such a simple broth made with the plants, herbs and game of the forests. His strength was returning with every drop. A well-fed fire glowed in the stone hearth as its flames licked around the side of the blackened stewpot.

'This is good,' he said. She smiled and

nodded. Her hair flowed freely over her shoulders. It was surprisingly clean for someone who lived in this harsh landscape. In fact, he noticed that there was not one spot of dirt on her. He assumed, by her appearance, that she used the river to bathe in far more often than most.

Again, the Kid studied the cabin carefully. It had one window. There was no glass in its frame, only a wooden shutter keeping the night chill out of the log construction. There was little inside the small cabin apart from a pile of kindling and some larger logs drying near the fire. A few dried fish hung on hooks in the smoke of the fire.

Whoever this quiet female was, Colorado knew that she was alone and had barely anything to her name. Yet she was willing to share what little she had with him.

Colorado finished his tasty broth and rested the cup on his knee. He then looked at his left hand and flexed the fingers.

Whatever magic she had used in the simple recipe, the pain had gone. His blue eyes looked across at her face.

'Who are you?' the Kid asked her again. 'Tell me, what's your name?'

She tilted her head but still did not answer. There was a look on her face that seemed to tell the large man that she either did not hear him or could not understand his simple question. He knew that many people who were isolated from their own kind could forget how to talk.

Was this the case with this beautiful girl? Could she have forgotten how to talk. Or perhaps she had never learned. Colorado leaned forward and placed his cup on top of the small table before her. She immediately jumped to her feet and used the hem of her ragged dress to lift the lid off the pot and refill the cup. Then she handed the cup back to her guest and returned the lid to the steaming pot.

She pointed to her own mouth and then the cup. She was using sign language to talk to him.

'You sure are a strange one,' the Kid said. He felt the warmth of the broth heating up the palms of his hands as its aroma filled his nostrils. 'I'm starting to think that maybe you can't hear a word I'm saying.'

She pointed to her ears and then nodded. She was telling him that she could hear.

'You ain't deaf?'

She shook her head again.

'Not deaf,' Colorado said as he sipped the broth. 'Can you speak?'

She pointed to her mouth and then shook her head.

Colorado knew then that she was mute. He wondered whether that was why she was here alone in the forest. Had she been abandoned simply because she could not talk?

He knew that the Sioux always took care of anyone who was different. But he had heard tales that many white folks were not as generous. Many tended to cast their disabled offspring out as if they had been cursed by the Devil. Could this handsome female be a victim of that sort of ignorance, he wondered?

'So you can't speak?' he asked her through the rising steam of the broth.

She gave a half-smile, then pointed to her mouth again and shook her head. The flickering flames of the fire danced on the tears in her eyes before she lowered her head.

Colorado swallowed hard and nodded.

'I'm sorry. I didn't mean to hurt you.'

He placed the cup on the table. Carefully he got to his feet and moved closer to the fire. He rested a hand on the stone fireplace. He looked down at her shining brown hair and knew that he was right.

She was an outcast.

Probably she had been discarded by one of the families back in Silver Springs when they discovered that she could not talk. He had been brought up to know that the Great Spirit loved all his children equally. It had come as a shock to him when he first realized that some of the so-called white Christians he had met since leaving his own people were capable of branding even children with being cursed. Some misguided souls even thought that being left-handed was an evil omen. He had heard people describe themselves as God-fearing. Colorado wondered what sort of god made people afraid of it. Even after so many years drifting amongst these people, he still could not understand them.

'I reckon I ought to give you a name,' he said.

Colorado watched her raise her head from her hands and look up at him. She was smiling again.

'Maybe I could call you Little Dove?'

She nodded.

'You like that, huh? I'm glad. I once knew another beautiful girl called that. That was a long time ago in another forest.'

Her small hand reached out and touched his.

'Did those folks in Silver Springs throw you out because you can't talk?' Colorado asked.

Again she nodded.

'I can understand them shooting at me because I might have been an outlaw, but to turn on a child don't make no sense.' The Kid sighed.

Little Dove shrugged. There was no anger or hatred in her beautiful soul. She accepted her life because she knew no other.

The Colorado Kid was not so forgiving. He

clenched both his fists as a rage rose up inside him. He moved to the window and stared through the gaps in the warped wooden shutter. He sighed heavily.

'And they call my people savages, Little Dove!'

THIRTEEN

The night still had a long life ahead of it before the eventual return of the first rays of the sun announced the arrival of a new day. Frank McCready had ridden into many towns in his time but none as eerily silent as Silver Springs was this day. It just did not seem normal. He drew back on his reins and looked all around him for signs of life. Apart from the dim glow of candles behind lace-draped bedroom windows, it was as if the entire population had obediently heeded a curfew.

McCready could see the distant light of glowing street-lanterns leading towards the heart of the small, well-tended town and wondered whether perhaps that was where most of the residents might be. He spurred his black stallion and continued deeper into the town in which he knew his chosen target lived.

With every step of his mount, McCready wondered whether Ben Baker did know of his imminent arrival. Or had he allowed the discovery of the dead body, far behind him, to blur his usually deadly judgement?

The stallion walked slowly down the centre of the narrow side streets as its master continued to look all around him for any signs of a trap.

There seemed to be none.

Was this one of those curious towns that actually went to sleep at sundown?

McCready began to relax as he drew closer and closer to the brightly illuminated Main Street. He hauled back on his reins again and stood in his stirrups. His eyes scanned every store-front until he was satisfied that there were no bushwhackers hiding in their shadows. He could see the light shining in the telegraph office and the small man sleeping at his desk.

He spun the horse around until he spotted the saloon and its bartender standing on the boardwalk sucking on a pipe. Light cascaded out from its windows and doors in all directions.

Even though there appeared to be no signs of danger, the town was too quiet for his liking.

He jabbed his spurs into the flesh of his mount and galloped across to the saloon. He stopped his horse and looked down at the plump man with the troublesome pipe.

'Where is everyone, barkeep?'

The man yawned and looked up as yet another match failed to light the tobacco in his pipe-bowl.

'Gone on a moonlit ride by all accounts, stranger.'

McCready leaned over and looked into the saloon's interior. It was empty. He straightened up and then pushed the brim of his Stetson up off his brow until it rested on the crown of his head.

'Everyone?'

'Not everyone,' the man answered. He struck another match along the seat of his pants and raised it to the pipe, only to see its flame blown out by the gentle yet persistent breeze. 'The bar girls have gone to bed alone. I'm talking about Baker and his boys. They rode off for the forest about a half hour back.'

McCready's eyes brightened.

'You talking about Ben Baker the lawyer?'

'Yep.' The man nodded.

'How many men has he got nowadays?'

'I ain't never counted them, son.' The bartender turned his back and struck another match. This time he managed to get its flame to the pipe. He started sucking. Smoke billowed from his mouth until an expression of satisfaction glowed in his large cheeks.

'Ten?'

'More like twenty.' The man puffed.

McCready swiftly dismounted and looped his reins over the hitching rail. He stepped up on to the boardwalk until he was standing beside the round man.

'You say that they've all gone riding? Ain't it a tad late to go riding?'

'Yep. You're right. I overheard the whole bunch of them gunslingers talking before they lit out. Baker's after some critter named McCready,' the bartender said as he led the way into the saloon. 'Seems like old Jeb Carter the mayor rode into the forest after this deadly gunfighter. Baker got himself into a real fit and decided to go after them. He wants to get them for some reason. I got the feeling that there'll be some killing before dawn. Leastways, that's what it sounded like to me.'

'Baker seems to be a pretty powerful man.'

'Yep. He is. That miniature army of his helps him stay that way, if you get my drift?'

'I get your drift.'

Frank McCready rested his left elbow on the bar counter and watched the large man make his way round to the other side until he was standing directly before a large mirror and countless whiskey-bottles.

'I'll have me three fingers of rye, barkeep,' he

said. He tossed a silver dollar into the plump hands.

'Sure enough.' The man picked up a bottle, pulled its cork and poured a generous measure of the fiery liquid into a glass tumbler. 'By the way, what's your name, stranger?'

'The name's Frank McCready!'

The bartender placed the whiskey bottle next the tumbler and swallowed hard as he gripped the pipe-stem firmly between his teeth.

'Not the same McCready that Ben's gone hunting?'

McCready downed the whiskey and then pushed the glass towards the shaking hands.

'I ain't sure who the hell he's chasing, barkeep. But it ain't me.'

The bartender automatically filled the glass again.

'They say you're a deadly killer.'

'Yep. I heard that too.' The smile on McCready's face grew broader as he picked up the tumbler and raised it to his lips. 'I reckon there must be something to that rumour, huh?'

The nervous bartender plucked another tumbler off the pyramid of gleaming glasses and poured himself a whiskey. He tossed the liquor down his throat and then exhaled heavily.

'What you figuring on doing, Mr McCready?'

Frank McCready turned his back on the

rotund man and stared across the expanse of soiled sawdust at the swing-doors of the saloon.

'I reckon I'll wait here until Ben Baker returns.'

'What then?'

McCready did not answer. He finished his drink knowing exactly what he would do. He would earn his blood-money.

FOURTEEN

Jeb Carter knew every inch of the large forested valley. He had once hunted beneath the well-nourished canopy of branches and fished the river's entire length. But that had been twenty or more years earlier, before the town of Silver Springs had developed to satisfy the miners. Carter had never sought out the precious ore that filled the mountainsides like other men. His family had been mountain people and he alone amongst them had ventured out into the surrounding territories. It had taken a long time for him to realize that there were no boardwalks paved with gold in even the largest of cities. If you wanted to discover happiness, sometimes it was better to search your own soul. For if it was not there, it could not be found anywhere.

This land was like a magnet. It had a power to draw its children back into its womb. He had returned and immediately been made the mayor of Silver Springs.

Yet things had not been the same. The innocence of this place had been lost somehow beneath the dirt and debris that the miners' pickaxes used to rip out the precious ore which they craved like a drug. But it was not the land's physical change that had alarmed the straight-talking man, it was the subtle unseen corruption that had strangled the people within the town's boundaries into submission. Carter knew that Ben Baker's power had crept like a cancer until he was taking a share of every dollar earned in Silver Springs. With his henchmen to enforce his will, Baker had ruled unchallenged for too long.

As he rode deeper into the forested valley, Carter was surprised that the forest itself had hardly altered at all. Maybe it was because the sun's vicious rays could not touch the ground here.

The valley was still as it had always been: almost untouched by the hand of man. Defiant and beautiful, its scars healed quickly in the moist atmosphere.

Jeb Carter remained standing in his stirrups as his strong hands steered the gelded chestnut. With every beat of his heart he wondered who and what Frank McCready really was. Was he actually here to kill Baker? Could he be the one man capable of ending the lawyer's reign of terror?

Curiosity drove him on and on.

He had ridden hard beside the river for more than an hour when he saw the one thing that he had not even suspected he might find. Evidence that, remarkably, there was still someone living in the forest.

At first the cabin's shape was obscured by the dark shadows and creeping ivy which covered almost all of its exterior. But the smoke which trailed heavenward from what was left of the stone chimney stopped him. He steadied the chestnut gelding and then hastily dismouted.

He gripped his reins tightly in his left hand and wondered whether the wounded man he sought might be inside the obviously occupied cabin.

One thing was certain. Somebody was.

Sparks drifted in the chimney's smoke like a million fireflies. For the first time since he had set out from Silver Springs, the white-haired man was afraid.

Unlike McCready, he was no gunfighter.

Carter touched the holstered gun grip as he studied the well-camouflaged cabin. Then he realized that if the man he sought was half as deadly as his reputation, he would not have the remotest chance to draw his Colt before

McCready killed him. Jeb Carter led his lathered-up mount closer and closer to the cabin.
Then a sudden movement just behind it made
him hesitate and kneel on the damp ground. He
kept his gun hand on the nose of the gelding. All
he needed now was for the animal to give away
his position before he had time to find cover.

He squinted hard and gazed at the shape
which continued to move behind the log cabin.
Although his eyes had adjusted to the darkness,
he still could not see anything clearly except
black shadows.

'What is that?' he whispered under his breath.

It was a terrified Carter who rose up and
summoned every last scrap of his courage before
he continued to walk forward. He knew that if
the hired killer was wounded, Frank McCready
might not be as good with his weaponry as he
usually was. On the other hand, Carter also knew
that a wounded animal, two- or four-legged, was
darn dangerous and totally unpredictable.

The ground was littered with nature's debris.
He prayed that if his boots did crush any twigs
their sound would not alert whoever it was inside
the cabin.

The wooden shutter on the solitary window
was shut but he could see a small shaft of light
escaping between the weathered cracks.

He continued to lead his tired mount ever

closer to the small cabin. With every cautious step he tried to see what it was that was moving beyond the bushes next to the ivy-covered walls.

Then he stopped and focused hard. For a few nerve-tingling seconds the darkness refused to reveal the its secret. Then he felt his heart starting to beat once more.

It was a horse!

A tall grey mare!

Carter's eyes darted all about him as another sudden terror filled his fearful mind.

If that was McCready's mount, then its master was close. Was he inside the cabin? Or was he out here waiting to take his revenge on anyone dumb enough to follow?

Silver Springs's mayor knew that there were countless trees all around him broad enough for even the stoutest of men to hide unseen behind.

He wondered whether it was he or his gelded chestnut who was breathing the loudest as he carried on walking straight at the cabin. He drew the .45 from its holster and cocked its hammer as quietly as he could. The last thing he wanted to do was kill this man if it was true that McCready was here to destroy the vicious Ben Baker.

Yet Carter had the feeling that if he did not have his gun in his hand when he eventually encountered McCready, he would surely die.

Men like the infamous hired assassin did not suffer fools gladly. At last, Carter released his grip on his reins and allowed his horse to graze as he moved across the last three yards up to the crude rotten door.

Light filtered through every warped plank of the door as Carter rested his terrified frame against it. He tried to stop his gunhand from shaking long enough to burst in and surprise the deadly McCready.

All he needed was to be able to get the drop on the man he had trailed to this spot. He needed enough time to convince McCready that he meant him no harm.

Would Frank McCready listen?

Could Carter manage to achieve that seemingly simple ambition without getting his own head blown off its shoulders?

The thought tortured Carter.

The mayor knew that he was a reasonably good shot, and had lived by hunting his food until he had left the mountains years earlier. But Carter had never faced a man like McCready. A man who only existed due to his lethal prowess with his weaponry.

Someone who killed to order.

The thought chilled him.

He pressed his ear up to the rotting door and listened. He could hear nothing except his own heart pounding inside his tight shirt like a drum.

Carter licked his dry lips, gritted his teeth, then leaned back until he felt as if his entire body was coiled like a spring. He threw his shoulder at the door. The damp wooden planks offered little resistance and broke into pieces before falling on to the floor of the cabin.

It came as a total surprise to the veteran mayor as he fell heavily into the cabin. Carter staggered and tried to maintain his balance with the gun gripped firmly in his sweating palm.

His eyes darted to the huge unarmed six-foot-six figure standing beside the fire. The Colorado Kid stared down at the crouching figure and raised an eyebrow.

The mayor steadied himself and suddenly realized that he was looking up at a man of gigantic proportions. He raised the barrel of the gun until it was aimed straight at the centre of the Colorado Kid.

'D . . . don't move a muscle, McCready!' he stammered. 'I don't want to shoot you. I want to talk.'

The Kid nodded.

'My name's Colorado, friend,' the Kid drawled. 'I listen a lot better when I ain't staring down the barrel of a forty-five.'

'I know who you really are!' Carter gulped. 'You're here to kill Ben Baker!'

'Ben Baker.' Colorado repeated the name. 'That name has been haunting me all day for some darn reason. What makes you think I'm going to kill him?'

'I seen a wire to Baker warning him that you're a hired killer, McCready!' Carter said.

The Kid watched as the terrified man straightened up.

'My name ain't McCready, friend. I ain't even heard of the critter. I told you, I'm called Colorado.'

Before Jeb Carter could respond, Little Dove sprang out from behind the mayor and kicked the gun from his sweating hand with her bare left foot. The weapon flew across the room and was caught in one of the Kid's huge hands.

Colorado studied the pistol before releasing its hammer and tucking it into his belt. He smiled at Little Dove as she moved around the stunned Carter. He then looked at the shorter man standing before him.

'You said you wanted to talk?'

Carter nodded.

'Yep. I . . . I did.'

'Then talk!' the Kid said.

FIFTEEN

It was a perilous route down the side of the tree-covered mountain into the misty dark valley. The trio had walked this same footpath countless times over the years that they had been mining the cave far above them, yet this time it felt different.

This time they were scared. So scared that they had brought their weaponry with them. The high-pitched noise of the wings of thousands of hungry bats swooping expertly between the tops of the trees was their only companion on the long dangerous descent.

But it was not the bats that frightened them. There was another sound down on the floor of the valley that they could not identify. It was that which unnerved them.

Only the moonlight gave any sense of reality to the sea of trees that surrounded the three miners as they edged their way down the narrow foot-trail towards the waterfall.

Buck Harper, Seth Marsh and Jonah Schmit were leading their small mule down towards the falls where they could fill their large water-bags. This was a routine that they had to repeat every few days, for there was no running water around the cave perched high on the side of the mountain.

All three men were armed with their scatter-guns, and ready for any trouble which might come their way. It had been a long time since anyone had been foolhardy enough to attempt to rob these men of their goods, but they knew that theirs was a dangerous occupation.

Harper stopped and waited for his two colleagues to catch up with him with the mule. The bearded men could sense that there was something wrong in the forest.

It had been several hours since they had heard the echoes of gunfire coming from the heart of Silver Springs and they knew that the giant whom they had met outside their cave must have ridden into another ambush.

'I don't like this, Buck,' Seth Marsh said as he hauled the mule alongside the alert older man.

'Me neither.' Jonah snorted. 'Things ain't right tonight. I got me a bad feelin'.'

'It's too darn quiet!'

'C'mon, boys,' Harper growled as he held his heavy weapon in both hands across his chest. 'Let's get us our water and get back up to the cave.'

The miners started towards the falls.

They could hear the strange noise which was growing louder with every passing moment. A noise which at first reminded the silver-miners of distant thunder.

'What is that, Seth?' Jonah asked nervously as they reached the banks of the river near the base of the waterfall. The water was like the froth on a glass of beer as the men removed the water-bags from the mule.

Seth Marsh looked up at the cloudless night sky above the top of the falls.

'It can't be thunder.'

Jonah stood beside the mule with his scatter-gun in his arms and slowly drew back its twin hammers until they locked.

'Horses?'

Buck held the large bag in the ice-cold water. He could feel it filling slowly. His eyes narrowed as they darted down the length of the river into the murky mist and black shadows.

'It is horses, Jonah,' he agreed. 'A whole bunch of the critters by the sound of it.'

'But who in tarnation would be loco enough to go riding in this forest at night?'

Seth swallowed hard.

'Could be Baker and his boys!'

'Maybe Colorado managed to get away from their guns earlier when we heard all that shootin'!'

The men dragged the heavy water-bags out of the foaming water and secured their stoppers. But they did not place the bags on to the mule. They lowered them on to the ground and then stared down into the darkness with more intensity.

'It must be Baker and his varmints!' Buck nodded. 'And they sound as if they're getting darn close.'

'Too close!'

'He might be wounded!'

'They fired enough bullets earlier.' Seth nodded. 'They must have hit him.'

'They must be after the giant,' Jonah added. 'We can't let them kill the giant, can we.'

Buck rubbed his beard down with his hands.

'We can't leave Colorado to take on that army alone, boys! Not if'n he's wounded.'

'That would be a sin.'

'Are we gonna just ignore this?'

All three looked at one another before speaking at exactly the same time.

'Nope!' they all said.

Harper led Schmit and Marsh along the river-bank towards the sound of horses. Each of the dishevelled men knew instinctively that there was only one way to defeat fear.

You faced it head on.

SIXTEEN

Ben Baker was like a general urging his troops on and on as they rode through the river-water towards the waterfall. He was careful to ride behind the front row of his hired henchmen, knowing that the two riders guiding their way with the blazing torches in their hands would more than likely be the first of McCready's targets. The Colorado Kid came out of the small cabin with Jeb Carter at his side. Both men had heard the sound of the horses' hoofs as they grew louder and louder along the valley floor.

'Baker must be bringing in all his men to finish you off, Colorado!' Carter said anxiously. 'Look! There they are! See their torches?'

The Kid pulled the mayor's gun from his belt and tossed it to the older man.

'Maybe it ain't me they're trailing, Jeb! By what you've told me of Ben Baker, he's the sort that wouldn't mourn your passing one bit either.'

Carter moved closer to the towering figure.

'You mean they might have trailed me in here, son?'

'Could be.' The Kid glanced away from the wall of water-spray which was rising up as the horsemen headed towards them. 'They might be following your trail. You thought about that?'

It was obvious that Carter had not even considered that Ben Baker might dislike him as much as he hated the lawyer.

'That means that we're both in trouble,' he said. 'They think that you're this McCready critter and Baker wants him dead. This might be a perfect opportunity for Baker to get my thorn out of his side too.'

'Two birds with one stone?' Colorado suggested as he hauled his Peacemaker from its holster.

'Yep!'

Little Dove came out of the cabin and grabbed the kid's sleeve. She pointed behind them in the direction of the falls. There was an urgency in her face that the Kid had never seen before.

'What's wrong, Little Dove?' Colorado asked.

She pointed again.

The Kid turned his head and squinted. He

could see the three figures of the silver-miners highlighted against the moonlit falls.

'Don't be afraid. I reckon I know them,' Colorado said in a soothing tone. 'They're my friends.'

'Who is that, Kid?' Carter asked, gripping his .45 in his hand. 'Whoever they are, they're carrying scatterguns by the looks of it.'

'They're miners I met up on the trail into Silver Springs, Jeb.' Colorado pointed up at the steep tree-covered slope. 'But I don't know why they're down here.'

The three gasping prospectors reached the side of the unmistakable Colorado and stopped to catch their breath. Buck Harper was the first to speak.

'I knew it was you, Kid!'

'Who else could it have been?' Seth Marsh sighed as he stared in the direction of Baker and his riders. 'We only ever met one giant.'

'And you is it!' Jonah piped up.

'They're getting too darn close!' Colorado muttered. He bit his lower lip thoughtfully.

'Like a bunch of hounds after a coon,' Buck growled. 'They got ya scent in their noses all right.'

Carter returned his attention to the riders heading towards them up the river. Their blazing torches chilled the half-dozen onlookers.

They were getting too close for comfort.

'I knew Baker was a wrong 'un, but I never imagined he was this bad!'

Suddenly, the riders opened fire. It was like a thunderstorm as the hot lead cut through the forest from their weaponry and deafened them. Colorado dragged Little Dove until she was behind his massive frame.

'Maybe this will slow them up!' Colorado drew his gun, aimed and fired. He watched one of the torchbearers fall off his mount and crash into the water.

'We have to get out of here, Kid!' Carter urged as more bullets tore through the brush. The trunks of the trees all about them exploded as bullets ripped into them.

'Reckon you're right, Jeb.' The Kid nodded and hastily led Little Dove through the brush to his mare waiting behind the cabin. He helped the girl on to the high saddle, then stepped into his stirrup and climbed up behind her until he was sitting on the bedroll.

He teased the grey mare a few feet closer to the cabin. Then he cocked and fired his Peacemaker again and again downriver.

Buck and his two companions knelt down with their scatterguns primed in their hands.

'You get going, Kid. We'll try and give ya cover!' the bewhiskered miner yelled out above the sound of the distant riders' gunfire. 'Get that little girl to safety! Now!'

Before Colorado had time to reply, the three miners opened up at Baker and his henchmen with their scatterguns. The buckshot blasted from the long barrels and stopped the riders in their tracks. Another two of the hired gunmen fell from their saddles and disappeared beneath the fast-flowing water.

Blinding flashes from both directions lit up the black forest.

Baker dragged his reins up to his chin and dismounted as he saw three more of his hired men topple from their saddles and crash into the river. It took less than a heartbeat for the remaining horsemen to follow suit and lead their mounts to the cover of the trees.

Jardine cranked the mechanism of his Winchester and started to fire ferociously at the cabin as the remaining men hid behind the trees.

'They've cut us in half, Mr Baker!'

The lawyer nodded and raised his own rifle.

'We got them cornered, Tom. There ain't nowhere for them to go unless they can swim up them falls like bunch of salmon!'

The hired gunmen's bullets continued to tear through the night air towards the handful of people beside the cabin.

'Get out of here!' Seth shouted. He dropped two more cartridges in the smoking barrels of his weapon and raised it to his shoulder. 'We're thinning 'em out.'

Jeb Carter swiftly mounted his gelding and yanked his reins hard around until he was facing the chiselled features of the Kid.

'But how are we gonna get out of here? I used to know this forest like the back of my hand, but it all looks so different now.'

Little Dove patted Colorado's left hand as it gripped the reins firmly. She pointed to their right and nodded.

'Is there a trail through that brush, young 'un?' Carter asked, bringing his mount along-side the grey.

'Reckon there must be, Jeb. Leastways, Little Dove reckons there is. C'mon!' Colorado slapped the palm of his large right hand and got the horse moving.

The chestnut was spurred into action.

Within seconds both horses were thundering through the darkness as the young woman used her keen instincts to guide them between the countless trees.

'Keep shootin', boys!' Buck yelled out at his pals.

Seth Marsh was about to load his gun again when he was knocked off his knees. He fell backwards. He tried to get up, then realized that there was a bullet hole in the middle of his chest.

'Gosh,' he gasped. 'That was sudden!'

Buck and Jonah stared in horror as they watched their old friend's head loll lifelessly to its side.

'Seth!' Jonah Schmit screamed out.

There was no reply.

'C'mon, Jonah!' Buck growled as more of Baker's men's venomous bullets ripped through the air towards them. 'Let's go kill us some varmints!'

Defying the bullets which rained at them, the pair of miners headed towards the guns of their enemy.

They had a score to settle.

SEVENTEEN

They knew that they had no time to waste. They had to try and find the safe passage out of the forested valley before Baker and his hired guns found them. The two horses galloped through the undergrowth, away from the bullets of their enemies. The moonlight filtered through the dense overhead branches just enough to allow the Colorado Kid to drive his grey mare on at breakneck speed.

With the sound of shooting still ringing in their ears, the two horsemen kept pushing their mounts as hard as they could in order to reach the place that Little Dove was indicating.

From this place they would find their way out of the valley and back to higher, safer ground.

But even after they had covered more than a mile through the trees and tangled brush, the sound of the shooting persisted.

Colorado dragged his reins back, stopped his horse and waited for the gelded chestnut to catch up with him. As Carter stopped his mount beside the snorting grey, the Kid turned and stared back through the moonlit forest.

'What's wrong, Kid?' Carter panted, steadying his eager horse. 'Why'd you stop?'

Colorado kept staring behind them with an intensity that few other men could equal.

'Hear that?'

'Sure do. The miners are still shooting it out with Baker and his bunch of vermin.'

The younger rider shook his head.

'Not that shooting, Jeb. Listen!'

Little Dove gestured with her hands, then nodded.

'Exactly!' Colorado said. He rested a hand on her slim shoulder and smiled. 'Little Dove hears it as well. Riders! Can't you hear the varmints?'

Jeb Carter stood in his stirrups, cupped the palm of his left hand to his ear, then screwed his eyes up and stared as hard as he was able.

'Nope. I don't see or hear nothing, Kid.'

Colorado looked at the brush ahead of them, then leaned over Little Dove's shoulder.

'How far is it to the trail out of here, Little Dove?'

She pointed at the moon and indicated that it had to move across the treetops before they would reach their safe route out of the valley.

The Kid looked at Carter.

'I figure that must mean about another half-hour or so.'

Carter shrugged.

'It's a darn long time since I measured time by the speed the moon moved across the heavens, son.'

Suddenly the sound of distant shots were drowned out by closer gunfire. The two riders looked behind them and could see the ten horsemen cutting their way through the trees. Then they saw the guns open up.

Flashes from the barrels illuminated the forest as the riders drove their mounts through the trees.

Red-hot tapers cut past them like crazed fireflies. Carter's chestnut spooked and reared up. The mayor fell off the back of his saddle and landed heavily against the trunk of a tree.

Colorado went to urge his grey after the skittish mount when another volley of shots blasted the bark off the side of the tree into his eyes.

For a few seconds he was blinded. He released his grip on his reins and covered his eyes with his hands.

'I can't see,' he yelled as he heard the thundering hoofs getting closer.

Little Dove lifted her leg over the mare's neck

and dropped to the ground. She grabbed at Colorado, as he sat helplessly on the back of the saddle and hauled him down. The grey bolted after the gelding as bullets skimmed off boulders and tore into trees.

Then she guided him to the safety of the trees.

When satisfied that the Kid's giant frame was safely behind a boulder, Little Dove pulled his six-shooter from its holster and held it in two hands.

With the bullets of Baker and his remaining henchmen still tearing up the ground all about them, she dragged the hammer back with both thumbs and aimed at the approaching horsemen.

She squeezed the trigger and was knocked backwards by the gun's kick as its .45 bullet went seeking its target.

Colorado kept rubbing his eyes, trying to extinguish the fire that had burned into them.

'Who's shooting? Is that you, Little Dove?'

She touched his cheek with her small hand as if to answer his question. Then she had to muster the strength of both thumbs again and try to pull back the hammer once more.

'Careful!' the Kid warned. 'You could shoot yourself. This gun's got a hair-trigger.'

She had no idea what he meant and carried on.

'Where are you, Jeb? Speak to me, old-timer.'

Carter groaned and rolled over until one of his hands touched the Kid's leg. He crawled up beside the seated figure as their female companion fired the Peacemaker again.

'What's going on, Kid?' asked the dazed Carter, struggling to shake the fog out of his cracked skull.

'We're in big trouble unless you can use that hogleg of yours.' Colorado replied.

Jeb Carter drew his weapon and leaned around the tree. He could see the riders taking cover a couple of hundred yards away from them.

'I see ten of the critters, Kid.'

Colorado at last managed to stop his eyes watering enough to lower his hands. He blinked hard and then felt soft hands on his face. It was Little Dove. She had plucked a handful of large leaves from beside them and crushed them until a white milky fluid covered her palms. She bathed his burning eyes with it until he began to regain his sight.

Carter fired three times and then ducked back behind the broad tree-trunk.

'You OK, Kid?'

Colorado blinked again.

'I am now, Jeb.'

He grabbed his long-barrelled gun off the

kneeling girl's lap and smiled at her. There was enough moonlight for her to see his teeth gleaming. She nodded as he cocked the hammer of his Peacemaker and levelled it at where he could see Baker and his cohorts' gunsmoke.

'Now it's time for some real shooting!' Colorado said. He fired his gun into the darkness.

The scream that filled their ears told the intrepid trio that his bullet had found one of their foes.

'Nine to go?'

'Reckon so, Kid.'

Carter looked all around them as his younger companion kept their adversaries at bay.

'I think I know where we are, Kid!' he exclaimed.

Colorado stopped firing.

'You recognize this place?'

The older man stood and bit his lower lip as he rested his spine against the tree-trunk. There was certainty in his voice as he answered.

'Of course! All we have to do is cut down that gully and there's an old mine tunnel that leads all the way through the mountain and right to Silver Springs!'

'What kinda tunnel, Jeb?'

'A big one. It used to be the best source of

118

silver in these parts, Kid.' Carter grinned. 'All we have to do is get there and we can lead the horses through it to safety.'

The Kid reloaded his gun.

'But what if this Baker critter and his men get there after we've entered? They could shoot us like sitting ducks!'

Carter raised an eyebrow.

'Baker and his scum don't even know it exists, Colorado. It was abandoned years before he ever set foot in these parts.'

Colorado looked down into the face of Little Dove.

'Is that what you were trying to tell us? Is that the trail out of here?'

She nodded.

The tall man waited for a lull in the shooting, and then urged his two comrades to start running. They did. The darkness of night gave them all the cover they required to reach their horses and head for the abandoned mine tunnel.

EIGHTEEN

Buck Harper and Jonah Schmit had never fought so many men with such hatred in their hearts before. They rested their weary bones on a fallen tree-trunk and stared at the bodies that were scattered around them like leaves after an autumn breeze. Even the darkness could not disguise the carnage that littered the river-bank.

The moon was casting its eerie light across the fast-moving water behind them. Even there, they could see bodies of men who had lived and died by the gun.

The saddle-horses of the gunmen had returned and found their fallen masters. They were standing around as if waiting for the blood-soaked corpses to come back to life and continue their ride into infamy.

Yet the two old silver-miners knew that none of

the men who lay around them would ever return to the land of the living again. They had drawn their last gun in anger. They had met men who were better than them and had lost their final battle.

Buck rubbed his bearded face with the tails of his neckerchief and somehow managed to come to terms with the fact that he and his friend had gotten the better of most of Baker's men and had chased off the rest.

'We managed to get through that tussle alive, Jonah.'

Jonah nodded and clung to the still-warm barrel of his scattergun.

'Yep. But Baker managed to squirm his way out of here before we got too close, Buck.'

Buck spat at the ground.

'Yeah, he sure did. Took a bunch of his vermin with him after the Kid, Carter and the girl, I reckon.'

'That's what the shooting must be over yonder, Buck!' Jonah looked up and stared into the dense brush. The sound of gunfire still rang out like ghostly echoes.

Buck rose to his feet and pulled his tattered pants up over his belly.

'Damn! I've been so upset over old Seth, I never even noticed the gunshots! Baker must have caught up with the Kid!'

Jonah got to his feet and tucked his scattergun under his arm.

'Are we goin' to do somethin' about that?'

'I think we are, Jonah.' Buck stomped his right boot on the ground. 'C'mon. Help me catch two of these nags. We'll go after Baker and settle with him permanent.'

'But I'm out of cartridges for my gun,' Jonah said.

Buck Harper pointed at the ground. It was littered with the arsenal of the dead gunmen.

'Rustle up two Winchesters and two six-shooters from these critters. They don't need them no more.'

Jonah beamed.

'Darn, I'd never have thought of that, Buck.'

Buck rolled his eyes.

'How come I knew that already, Jonah?'

NINETEEN

Jeb Carter had been right. The abandoned cave was exactly where he had said it would be. But decades of neglect had allowed the forest to reclaim its entrance. Tangled vines covered the once large mouth of the silver-mine's tunnel, making it indistinguishable amongst the rest of the forested mountainside.

The chestnut gelding was aimed down into the dark, deep gully by the skilled horseman. Carter glanced over his shoulder and watched the Colorado Kid sitting behind Little Dove on the tall grey mare following him.

Carter had been the first to spot the cave that nature had tried to hide from human eyes. Yet it was more from memory than any clear clue that the shadowy undergrowth offered his tired eyes.

He dismounted and started to drag at the barricade of twisted brush as the Colorado Kid reined in and looked on.

'What you doing, Jeb?'

The older man continued to work feverishly.

'This is the tunnel, son! Help me!'

Little Dove remained in the saddle as her tall riding companion slid off the back of his grey mare and rushed to the sweating Carter's side.

'Are you sure?'

'Yep. It's here!'

'I'll have to take your word for it!' The Kid sighed trustingly.

Colorado tore at the vines with his huge hands. Within seconds both men felt a cool breeze brush their faces. A breeze that had travelled the length of the silver-mine tunnel from far above them.

'How long does it take to get through this tunnel, Jeb?'

'It's at least a half-mile, if my memory serves me right,' Carter answered. 'But it has been an awful long time since I walked through here.'

They worked like men possessed until they had created a gap in the tangle of vegetation large enough for them to lead their horses through.

'Reckon this is big enough, Kid?' Carter asked, straining to see anything in the blackness.

Colorado had to use his hands to try and find an answer to his friend's question. He patted the strange, twisted liana and tried to judge how wide the gap they had created was, for he could see nothing clearly.

'Feels OK to me.' Colorado glanced back at their horses standing side by side half-way down the gully. The few shafts of moonlight which managed to defy the dense canopy of branches high above them, highlighted Little Dove as she sat on the long-legged grey mare. 'Bring the horses here, Little Dove.'

Both men watched as the young woman reached across from her mount and grabbed the reins of Carter's gelded chestnut. She then started to encourage the horses to descend into the blackness.

Suddenly the spine-chilling sound of a shot echoed around them. Both men froze to the spot for a brief moment as they realized that once again their dogged pursuers had caught up with them.

The sound of more shots rang out as the two figures saw the hot lead rip through the brush above them.

'Get down here, Little Dove!' Colorado yelled out at the tiny figure.

Carter and Colorado ran up the gully, drew their guns from their holsters, cocked their hammers and fired into the distance. They could see the blinding flashes of gunfire a few hundred feet away from them. Carter and the Kid returned fire and then slapped the tails of their mounts. The two horses trotted down into the blackness below them.

A volley of shots tore all around the gigantic figure of the Kid, who gritted his teeth and fanned the hammer of his Peacemaker. He heard the distant cries of men that his well-grouped bullets had found.

'Reckon I just thinned them varmints down again, Jeb!'

'C'mon, son!' Carter said. He grabbed the Kid's sleeve. 'Let's get to that tunnel and high-tail it out of this devilish place.'

Colorado did not require a second to think about his pal's suggestion. He turned and followed the older man down towards their horses.

'You better get down, Little Dove,' the Kid said, placing his huge hands around her tiny waist.

As his fingers almost circled her waist Colorado realized something was wrong.

The warmth of blood greeted his grip.

Colorado felt her falling from the high saddle helplessly towards him. His large arms caught her as if she were no heavier than a feather. He cradled her lifeless body and walked towards Jeb Carter who was gathering up the reins of his mount and was about enter the tunnel.

Even the darkness could not hide the grim, shocked expression carved into Colorado's features.

Carter searched his vest pockets and found a box of matches.

He struck one and held its flame over the body of Little Dove as she lay in the Kid's arms.

Both men stared at the blood-soaked chest of the young woman. The exit wound of the bullet was big and cruel. It had gone right through her.

'She's gone, son,' Carter said as the match flame flickered and then extinguished.

'They back-shot her, Jeb!' Colorado muttered as he lowered the limp body on to the wet grass between them. 'They killed her for no darn reason.'

'I know. But there's nothing we can do for her now except leave her here.' Carter rested a hand on the Kid's arm. 'If we survive until sun-up, we can come back and give her a decent burial.'

The Kid inhaled deeply and plucked the reins of his horse off the ground. He trailed the older man towards the mouth of the hidden tunnel. As Carter led the gelding into the blackness Colorado paused for a second and stared at where he had laid the body.

'Thanks, little lady. I owe you.'

He led the grey into the tunnel and then

pulled the vines back over the opening until it was once again covered. He started to lead his horse after Carter.

'And I always pay my debts!'

TWENTY

The six riders spurred their horses and thundered through the dark side streets, heading for the centre of the town. It was a desperate and confused Ben Baker who led what was left of his hired gunmen back into Silver Springs. Blood ran freely over his horse's neck from the bleeding bullet hole just beneath his left collar-bone.

There was a fear inside the lawyer which had grown over the previous couple of hours. Baker and his followers had tried to find the two men who had matched the accuracy of his highly paid gunmen, but somehow Carter and the man he still thought was Frank McCready had eluded them.

They had completely disappeared.

Even wounded, Baker's calculating legally trained brain knew that men could not simply vanish into thin air. He had led his men back to

Silver Springs knowing that wherever his quarry had gone, they had to return to this town eventually.

It was his intention to be waiting for them when they did.

The six horses cantered to a halt outside the well-lit saloon and drew alongside the black stallion tethered to one of the hitching rails.

Baker threw his right leg over the head and neck of his lathered-up mount, then slid to the ground. He touched the wound and flinched as he stared in disbelief at the red tips of his gloved fingers.

'What is going on here?' His question seemed to be aimed at every one of his confused men as they too dismounted all around him.

'We should have waited until daybreak, Mr Baker,' Jardine said in a hushed tone. He circled the rear of his horse and stared at the magnificent stallion at the end of the hitching rail.

'Tom's right! We was buzzard-bait out there!' Chill Smith snarled as he searched his gunbelt for bullets to refill the red hot chambers of his guns.

The bald Grover Pyle rubbed his gleaming head with the palm of his hand and coughed. He sat down on the edge of the boardwalk and looked at the other gunmen who stood silent beside their mounts.

'I'm for quitting this darn town!' he said.

The other men mumbled in agreement and nodded, their eyes keeping a close watch on Baker. None had any stomach for continuing this fight but feared the lawyer who they knew was capable of turning on even his closest allies.

'I thought that apart from old Jeb, there was only that McCready varmint in the valley!' Baker announced. He walked to Tom Jardine's side and rested a hand upon his shoulder, to steady himself.

'There had to be at least a half-dozen of the critters near the falls, Mr Baker,' Jardine said, staring at the stallion with grime-filled eyes.

Baker spat and searched his pockets vainly for a cigar.

'You're right! At least six. We rode straight into their guns like lambs to the slaughter!'

'Yep,' Jardine agreed.

'You got a smoke, Tom?' Baker asked.

'Nope. Left my tobacco-pouch and makings in the saloon earlier with one of the girls.' Jardine stepped forward and ran a hand along the flank of the black horse. Its coat gleamed in the lantern-light. 'You got any idea who owns this stallion, Mr Baker?'

Ben Baker continued to hold his hand against the bleeding wound and walked to his top gun's side. His eyes narrowed as he studied the stallion.

'I've never seen it before.'

Jardine moved along the animal and stared at the expensive saddle. It was adorned with engraved silver diamond shapes. No simple drifter or cowboy could ever have afforded anything like this, he thought.

'Are you sure that was McCready we trailed into the valley, Mr Baker?' Jardine asked as his eyes spotted something on the saddle fender.

Baker lowered his head.

'What? Why are you asking me such a dumb question? That had to be McCready, didn't it? The wire I had from Twin Forks said that he was headed to Silver Springs. If it wasn't McCready, then who the hell was it?'

Jardine lifted the fender up, wiped some trail dust off it and stared at the silver inlaid letters: F.M.

'Whoever that was we just got ourselves tangled up with, I reckon it weren't McCready.'

Baker strode to the stallion and stared at the initials on the saddle fender.

'Oh, dear Lord!' the lawyer gasped. 'What the hell is going on here?'

Tom Jardine released the fender, then turned around and stared up at the saloon doors. He gulped and quickly checked that his guns were loaded.

'I got me a feeling that McCready is in there, Mr Baker. If'n he is, we're in real bad trouble.'

Baker moved away from the stallion and waved his right arm frantically at the four other men.

'We made a mistake, boys. The real Frank McCready is in the saloon.'

Chill Smith nodded. A twisted smile etched across his youthful features.

'Then let's go kill the dude!'

Grover Pyle shook his head and grabbed the reins of his horse.

'You can go get yourself killed if that's what makes you happy, sonny. But I'm ready to head on out.'

Pyle stepped into his stirrup and hoisted his heavy bulk on to his horse. He steadied the mount and glanced down at the faces of the other five men.

'I quit, Mr Baker. It's bin darn nice working for you but I already come face to face with one McCready and got my ass kicked. I sure ain't gonna face another one. 'Specially when you say that this one is the real one. *Adios.*'

Before Pyle had time to turn his mount away from the front of the saloon, two other gunmen hastily mounted their sweat-soaked horses as well.

Baker gritted his teeth and drew his gun.

'I'll kill you, Grover!'

Pyle looked down at the wounded lawyer. He suddenly did not care what happened to him. He was a beaten man.

'You can shoot me if'n that's what you wanna do, Mr Baker. But I still ain't facing no hired killer. And neither should you. You ought to get smart and head on out of this town too. Reckon our luck just ran out.'

Baker lowered his gun and watched the three horsemen spur their mounts and gallop away from the saloon.

Smith looked at his boss's face hard and long.

'C'mon, Mr Baker. Let's go kill that McCready critter!'

Ben Baker said nothing as Jardine stepped beside him and nudged his elbow. The lawyer looked at Jardine, then turned his head in the same direction as the gunman's eyes.

He felt his heart skip a beat as he saw the awesome image of the deadly assassin, clad entirely in black leather standing in the frame of the saloon's doors with the glowing light behind him.

'Reckon that must be him, Mr Baker!' Jardine said out of the corner of his mouth. 'He sure looks like he's serious about his job. Look at that fancy shooting-rig he's sportin'!'

Ben Baker inhaled deeply.

'Are you Frank McCready?'

McCready released his grip on the swing-doors and stepped out on to the boardwalk. His eyes seemed to glow in the lantern-light as he studied his prey and the two men who flanked the bleeding figure of the lawyer.

'So I was right! You were expecting me, Baker!'

Baker licked his dry lips and felt the gun in his hand getting heavier and heavier.

'I was told that you were coming here to kill me!'

'Who told you?'

'A friend in Twin Forks!'

'Has this friend got a name?' McCready moved to the edge of the boardwalk and studied the three men below him, a few yards away from the tethered horses.

'The wire was unsigned.'

'How many friends you got in Twin Forks? I figure that they must be pretty thin on the ground.'

Baker suddenly realized that the hired killer was correct. He had only one friend in the Dakota town.

'Reckon it must have been Ward Slye. Him and me were pals a long time ago.'

McCready flexed his fingers. His hands rose slowly from his hips until they hovered above the grips of his matched pair of guns.

'Slye! I know him. He's a rancher. Nice man.'

'Will you go back and kill him?' Chill Smith asked eagerly as if he was starting to admire the man who faced them.

'Nope. I only kill men I'm paid to kill, son. There ain't no profit in wasting lead.' McCready looked in turn at Smith and Jardine. 'But I do make exceptions. If you boys think you can join in to help your boss, it'll be a mistake. Your last mistake.'

Chill Smith began to shake. His small brain could not work out what he ought to be doing next. His type of back-shooter liked killing and Chill had earned his salary many times, but this was different. He was facing a man who was a hired assassin, unlike his usual opponents. McCready was the epitome of a true gunfighter. There was not one scrap of emotion in either the face or the voice of the man.

McCready was giving Smith and Jardine the chance to desert their paymaster. Not because he liked them, but because he had only been paid to kill Baker. That was his agreement and to kill anyone else was simply uneconomical.

'You mean that me and Tom could walk away from here without you killing us?' Smith asked.

McCready nodded. 'Yep!'

'And if we stay to help our boss?'

'You'll both die!' came the simple response.

An ashen-faced Chill Smith had suddenly lost every drop of his courage. The youngster felt his heart pounding as fear raced through his entire body. He could not take his eyes off McCready's hands as they flexed a few inches above the pearl-handled gun-grips. Smith tried to speak but it was as if some unseen hand was squeezing his throat. Sweat trickled down his face from the hatband of his Stetson and ran into his unblinking eyes. As he moved towards his horse he felt a hand grab his shirt collar.

'Where you goin', yella-belly?' Tom Jardine snarled as he stopped Smith's attempt to reach his horse. 'You always talk big, but when it comes time to prove yourself, you wanna run like a scared rabbit. Stay and fight!'

'Let go of me, ya dumb fool,' Smith managed to yell before breaking free of his companion's vicelike grip. 'Look at him, Tom. He's ready to kill us all. I ain't stayin' here to back up Baker. He ain't worth it.'

Baker raised his weapon and aimed it straight at Smith. He squeezed the trigger and watched as the bullet shattered the youngster's skull. The body was lifted off its feet and landed beneath the hoofs of the closest of their tethered horses. The spooked animal bucked and crushed what was left of Smith's carcass into the ground.

Jardine wiped the blood from his face and then stared at the emotionless lawyer.

'What you do that for?' he screamed.

'Shut the hell up!' Baker snapped. Then he returned his attention to the startled McCready. 'Chill was a coward. You want to join him in boot hill, Tom? Well, do you?'

'I'll back up your play, Mr Baker.' Jardine shrugged and moved away from the blood stained ground until he was standing next to the furious lawyer.

Ben Baker lowered his smoking weapon and smirked.

'Good!'

Frank McCready inhaled the gunsmoke into his nostrils and tried to understand why the lawyer had killed one of his own men for no reason.

'No wonder Brewster Doyle wants you dead, Baker.'

Ben Baker licked his lips again and squared up to the hired killer on the boardwalk. He knew that he still had one way of settling this without having to risk the wrath of McCready's matched Colts.

'Whatever Doyle paid you, I'll double. Hear me? Whatever Doyle gave you I'll double, McCready! All you have to do is ride out of Silver Springs.'

'No deal!' McCready snapped. 'When Frank McCready makes an agreement, he honours it!'

'What does your sort of vermin know about honour?' Baker raged. 'You're just a gun for hire! No better than the misfits who work for me.'

McCready's eyes darted to look at Jardine before returning to the lawyer.

'Seems to me that you're a tad shy on misfits at the moment, Baker.'

Tom Jardine still could not believe that Baker had killed the youngest member of their once numerous gang. He could not stop shaking his head and mumbling quietly into his bandanna. Every one of his senses told him to walk away but he remained rooted to the spot. Even though Baker did not realize it, he still had one loyal employee.

'Then I reckon we have to settle this, McCready!' Baker piped up. His thumb pulled back the hammer of the gun at his thigh.

McCready sighed heavily and lowered his head so that he was concentrating on the two men. His fingers moved constantly as they hovered above the grips of his holstered guns.

'Make your play, gents!'

Suddenly the sound of horses approaching echoed around the wooden buildings and drew the attention of Frank McCready. He glanced up and looked over the heads of the two men below him in the street. He saw the pair of horses coming into view, carrying Colorado and Carter.

Baker tilted the barrel of his weapon until it was aimed at the leather-clad figure. He squeezed its trigger.

The deafening noise of the gun being fired came as a total shock to Frank McCready. He had taken his eyes off Ben Baker for a mere few seconds, but that had been too long.

As the acrid stench of gunsmoke filled his lungs he felt himself being hit backwards by the sheer force of the bullet. His spine crashed into the wall of the saloon before he felt the blood pumping from his middle.

'You skunk!' McCready muttered.

Baker laughed, raised his arm swiftly and cocked the hammer again.

'Eat lead, McCready!'

McCready's hands went for his guns but two more shots ripped into him in quick succession. His legs buckled and gave way from beneath him. His eyes glazed before he toppled over and landed face first on the boardwalk.

'You killed him !' Jardine said in total disbelief. 'You killed Frank McCready!'

The Colorado Kid and Jeb Carter drew back on their reins when they saw the lantern-lit scene ahead of them. Desperately they tried to stop their mounts.

Baker and Jardine swung around and stared at the two horsemen coming towards them. The lawyer cocked the hammer of his gun again and aimed its smoking barrel at Jeb Carter.

'Get that gun out of its holster, Tom!' he ordered. 'We ain't finished yet. Not by a long shot!'

Baker fired and watched as the gelded chestnut crashed into the street dust. Jeb Carter went over the horse's head and rolled head over heels.

Colorado steadied his horse, drew his Peacemaker and returned fire through the almost blinding haze of gunsmoke. Out of the corner of his eye he could see that both Carter and his chestnut mount were lying motionless next to the hoofs of his grey mare.

'You OK, Jeb?' the Kid shouted as bullets flew past him. He leapt to the ground beside the fallen Carter and knelt down next to the crumpled figure. He continued firing as his left hand shook the mayor.

The older man started to groan.

'You OK?' the Kid asked above the sound of the gunfire that filled Main Street.

'Quit shaking me, Kid! I ain't dead!' Carter growled as he felt his bones being rocked inside his weathered frame.

'Hang on to that thought!' Colorado said. A bullet ripped through his shirt and skinned his ribs. He winced in agony and screwed up his eyes. 'Damn!'

He then saw Baker and Jardine rushing away from the saloon toward the large building with the word CRUCIBLE painted on its façade.

Colorado staggered to his feet, emptied the empty shells from his gun and started to fill its chambers with the last six he had on his gunbelt.

'What you doing, Kid?' Carter asked as he managed to get his wind back and scramble off the ground.

Colorado gritted his teeth and snapped the chamber of the Peacemaker shut. He cocked its hammer and headed for the building into which he had watched the two men rush.

'It ain't over yet, Jeb!'

TWENTY-ONE

Before Jeb Carter had time to steady himself, he saw the Colorado Kid run across the wide street towards the Crucible Building and kick his way through its locked glass-panelled doors. Glass shattered into a million slivers as the tall man charged his way into its dark unlit hallway.

The Kid dropped on to one knee and studied the unfamiliar and very dark corridor ahead of him. He held his long-barrelled Peacemaker across his chest and allowed his eyes to adjust to the lack of light. He rose back to his full height and slowly began to walk past a number of offices, towards the flight of stairs at the end of the corridor.

His keen hearing could make out the men far above him on the next floor, frantically searching for something.

Colorado wondered what could have made

them enter this place when they could have gone for their horses. Then it dawned on him that the small card he had taken from the dead man near the river had said that Ben Baker's offices were here in the Crucible. This was the Crucible!

Baker must have led his last gunman here to get more ammunition or the money he had managed to fleece from the people of Silver Springs over the previous few years.

Or both!

The Colorado Kid gritted his teeth and continued making his way through the building. There was a fire inside him that he had never known before. It was driving him on and on.

It was not simply anger, it was something far more dangerous that that. It was revenge!

The moccasins allowed him to move without making any sound whatsoever through the building. When he reached the foot of the stairs he screwed up his eyes and peered up into the darkness.

As Colorado began to ascend the stairs, three at a time, he could not see a thing. The smell of kerosene filled the building and he realized that Baker and Jardine had smashed every one of the lamps that would have filled the building with light.

He knew that the lawyer and Jardine were

afraid. They had call to be. For they were now the hunted, not the hunters. Colorado held his breath and tried not to inhale the fumes which rose from the kerosene-soaked steps beneath him. The Kid felt glass fragments from the broken lamp-bowls crush beneath his large feet as he continued to make his way up towards the dark second storey.

Half-way up the staircase, Colorado paused.

He might not be able to see anything, he thought, but he could sure hear the two men frantically searching for ammunition in Baker's office.

Colorado knew that to continue up to the top of the flight of steps would more than likely prove suicidal. Baker and Jardine would already have heard the Kid smashing his way through the locked doors and into the building.

They would be waiting to fill him with lead as soon as he reached the second floor of the Crucible.

Then it dawned on him. He had to use every one of the advantages that he had been blessed with. His height and his unmatched hunting ability might just prove the deciding factors in this strange unholy situation.

The Kid holstered his gun and looked straight up at the high ceiling above him. There were few men in the West who could have equalled

Colorado's incredible reach and manage to find the wooden joist above him. But the huge hands and powerful fingers of the stretching giant not only found the joist, but were able to get a good enough hold on it for him to drag himself up into the air off the staircase.

The Kid used every muscle in his arms and shoulders to climb up the wall. He swung back and forth until his feet located the moulded wooden beading which trimmed the stairwell. Like a mountaineer scaling a perilous peak, the Kid ascended into the darkness until he found a wooden ledge strong enough to support his weight.

Colorado looked around the corner of the high wall that he was clinging to like a spider, and stared into Ben Baker's office through the open doorway. Shafts of moonlight poured into the office from the large window behind the busy lawyer.

'Keep your eyes on the stairs, Tom!' Baker ordered Jardine as he scooped out the bags of money from his office safe. 'That big *hombre* with Carter has gotta show himself sooner or later. When he does, part his hair between his eyes!'

'Sure enough, Mr Baker.' Jardine nodded as he gripped his cocked gun his his hand. 'I'll kill him as soon as I see him.'

'When we're finished here, we'll go out

through the back of the building and head for the livery stables. We'll take two fresh horses and head for the state line,' Baker said as he continued to fill his bag with money.

The Colorado Kid bit his lip.

He had to do something that would enable him to surprise the two men. His mind raced. He knew that if he tried to move from the precarious perch, Jardine would fill him with lead before his feet touched the floor.

He inhaled deeply through his nose and then screwed up his eyes as his head filled with kerosene fumes. He shook his head, then raised an eyebrow.

That was it!

The entire stairwell was soaked in the lamp-oil.

Fire! He thought. That would get their attention away from him.

Colorado pushed his fingers into his pants pocket and pulled out a small metal matchbox. Using only one hand, he opened the box and pulled out a long red-tipped matchstick. He dragged his thumbnail across it and watched as the flame ignited.

'What was that?' Jardine asked as he saw the reflection of the flame on the opposite wall of the stairwell.

Baker looked up from his safe.

'What was what, Tom?'

Jardine ventured a few steps out into the corridor.

'I seen a glow. On the wall.'

Colorado knew that he had to act before the last of Baker's gunmen got too close. He held the match until nearly all of its length was consumed in flame.

Then he dropped it down to the foot of the stairs below him.

The Kid watched as the match fell into the kerosene.

Suddenly the entire stairwell erupted into flames. The fire spread in every direction within a split second of the match hitting the fluid. To his surprise, the flames started to climb up the wall of the stairwell. Then he could see the shattered oil-lamps dotted every few yards up the wall. The walls were also soaked in kerosene from where Baker and Jardine had smashed them as they made their way up to his office.

The heat and smoke engulfed the confined area.

'Fire!' Jardine shouted out in horror.

Baker secured his moneybag and hauled it off the floor. He turned and stared in disbelief at the raging inferno.

'The varmints are trying to burn us out of here!' he exclaimed.

Jardine backed up into the lawyer. He was terrified.

'We can't get out! The fire's eaten up the stairs! What we gonna do?'

As choking smoke filled the second floor of the building, the Kid swung around and dropped from the high joist. He landed on both men, sending them cartwheeling across the floor.

With flames spreading like flowing water over the wooden flooring, the three men grappled furiously. Jardine somehow managed to slip from beneath the massive frame of the Kid and ran back into the office.

Jardine desperately tried to open the window but it would not budge. He grabbed hold of Baker's desk chair and threw it with all his might at the stubborn window. As the padded leather went straight through the panes of glass, a sudden gust of night air rushed through the building.

The gunman scrambled out on to the high balcony and saw two of the miners dismounting below him, next to Jeb Carter. He aimed his gun down at the men and fired.

His bullet just missed Buck Harper.

Jonah Schmit raised his Winchester and fired back at Baker's last henchman.

The miner's bullet was deadly. Tom Jardine

staggered and then toppled over the balcony. The three men watched as the body landed heavily on the ground.

Suddenly, Colorado and Baker came through another window and landed only a few yards from the spot from where Jardine had fallen.

Their clothes were alight, but neither man seemed to notice as they fought like wildcats across the length of the high balcony.

Colorado ducked as Baker tried to land the barrel of his Colt on the taller man's skull. As the Kid was low, he threw a hefty right fist into the lawyer's midriff. Baker went crashing into the flaming wall, sending a plume of smoke into the night air.

As Colorado moved in again, Baker smashed the grip of his gun across his chin, but Colorado continued to punch his opponent to the body.

Then Baker kicked out and sent the Kid flying over the wooden rail of the balcony.

Somehow, the Kid managed to grab hold of the top of the rail. Just as he raised his right foot up and started to climb back, Baker fired.

The bullet hit the rail and a million splinters of red-hot debris exploded into the face of the Colorado Kid.

The Kid released his grip and clutched his face. Before he knew what was happening, he was falling to the ground.

Every ounce of wind was knocked out of his body as he landed hard beside Jeb Carter and the two miners. Carter used his Stetson as a makeshift bucket and doused water from a trough over the burning clothes of the stunned Kid.

As Colorado's eyes cleared, he saw Baker leaning over the balcony with his deadly Colt .45 in his hand.

'Look out, boys!' the Kid yelled out as he struggled to get back to his feet.

Then a gust of wind seemed to come from nowhere. It fanned the red flames of the blazing building. Before any of the four men on the ground could do a thing, a huge ball of fire spewed out from the high windows and wrapped around the lawyer.

Colorado and his companions watched as Ben Baker's blazing figure ran the length of the balcony before being devoured by the red-hot inferno.

Within seconds the building was starting to collapse.

Carter shook his head.

'You all right, Kid?'

There was no answer. Colorado just stood watching the vicious flames. He would not move until he was convinced that Baker was really dead. He would wait all night so that he could see the charred remains with his own eyes.

Only then would he believe that it was over for good.

FINALE

For the first time for years the streets of Silver Springs were filled with men and women who were suddenly no longer afraid of what they might encounter. It seemed that the news of Ben Baker's death had spread like wildfire through the town's entire population within a few short hours. Not one tear was shed. The new day had arrived too late to save the mute beauty the Colorado Kid had briefly called Little Dove. The brilliant sun had risen over a bloodstained landscape, and for the majority it was as if they had been saved from the grip of a tyrant.

The mysterious giant rider had rid Silver Springs of Baker and his men. They wanted to thank him but all of them could see that the Kid had not taken any pleasure in the deed.

'You headed on out, Kid?' Jeb Carter asked. He stepped down off the boardwalk and paced across to the livery stable where the tall man had placed the blanket on the grey mare's back.

'Yep,' Colorado answered briefly.

Carter looked at the Kid's bruised face. His eyes then moved down. He saw the dried blood-stains which covered Colorado's clothing.

'You had the doc look at them injuries?'

'No call to trouble a doctor, Jeb.' The Kid ran a hand down the neck of the faithful animal. His blue eyes gazed upon the scores of curious people that were watching him from every direction. He had never seen so much curiosity before in one place and it made him uneasy.

'Where are you from, originally?' Carter asked, resting his rear on the edge of a water-trough. 'Some of these folks have remarked that you got the look of an Indian about you. Others say that you must be from Canada where they say men grow as big as the trees. What's the truth, Colorado?'

The Kid paused for a second.

'I don't know, Jeb.'

'Huh? We all know where we hail from.'

Colorado continued to gather his saddle gear together.

'Not me. I was found by the Sioux. They raised me. But none of them ever told me where they found me.'

'They didn't?'

'Nope. Reckon they didn't see the need to go into any detail about that. They adopted me as one of their own. That was good enough.' The Kid checked his Peacemaker, then holstered it and placed the safety loop over its hammer. 'I guess they reckoned that sometimes a man can know too much about himself. I guess they were right.'

Carter rubbed his freshly shaven chin.

'How come you left them? I'd have thought that leaving one world to go into another might be darn tough.'

'It was but I got curious. Thought that maybe I might one day find out who I really am.' The Kid placed the bridle over the mare's head and hung the reins on the horse's mane. 'But all I've ever found, so far, is trouble.'

'You ever been back to the Sioux?' Carter asked.

'Yep. But they were gone.' Colorado sighed. 'Every one of them had just vanished into thin air. It's as if they never existed at all.'

Carter recalled the newspaper stories he had read about the fate of the Sioux and several other tribes which the cavalry thought were involved in Custer's demise. He could tell that the Kid knew nothing about those events and decided it was best he remained ignorant of the brutal facts.

'Buck and Jonah are in the saloon being treated like kings for their part in last night's fracas.' Carter grinned. 'You ought to join them and have a few drinks.'

'Never had the taste for firewater, Jeb. But you can tell them that I think they're good men and I'm sorry about their friend.'

Jeb Carter stood and stared into the eyes of the man who towered over him and every other living soul in the town. This was the first time he had studied the Kid in daylight and he was surprised.

'Damn. I never noticed it before but you've got the bluest eyes I ever seen,' he gasped. 'I reckon you ain't no Indian with eyes that colour.'

'Blue like the sky!' the Kid added. 'That was what the Sioux said. They said my eyes were the colour of the sky. Reckoned it was powerful medicine.'

The older man circled around the handsome horse and watched the obviously injured Kid continuing to prepare the animal for a long ride.

'You could stay here in town until you're rested up, son,' Jeb Carter suggested. 'You've earned the right. We'll feed you and your horse until you've a mind to leave.'

Colorado shook his head.

'I've a mind to leave now. To be honest, I don't really like this place, Jeb.'

'So you'll just ride out?' Carter sighed. 'Ride out and head for God knows where?'

Again the Kid nodded.

'Yep. But first I have something to do.'

'What you got to do that's so important, Colorado?'

'It don't matter none.' The Colorado Kid could tell that Carter and the rest of the towns-people wanted him to remain. Maybe they thought he might protect them should other men like Ben Baker ever ride into their remote town again.

The Kid had never looked for trouble in his entire life, yet when he rode into Silver Springs, that was exactly what he had found.

Trouble and brutal pain.

Now he had other things on his mind. Things which would take him back to the small gully in the forest with a pickaxe and shovel. His bruised and bloodied frame cared little for what was happening around him as he hauled the heavy saddle over the blanket on the back of his grey mare and secured the cinch straps.

'I'll miss you, son,' Carter admitted as he watched the large hands strap the bedroll and saddle-bags to the cantle. Colorado then slid the pickaxe and shovel beneath the fenders.

He stepped into his stirrup and mounted the grey mare slowly. He gathered up the slack in his reins and looked down into the face of the older man.

'I'll miss you, Jeb. Apart from the miners, you're one of the few varmints around here who didn't try and kill me.'

Carter looked at the shovel and pickaxe.

'You ain't thinking of going looking for silver are you, Colorado?'

The Kid did not reply. He simply tapped his heels against the sides of the horse and urged the grey on. The mare started to walk away from the livery stable, then gathered pace.

He aimed his mount for the mine tunnel that he and Carter had used during the hours of darkness to reach Silver Springs. He was going to keep a promise he had made and was returning to the forested valley to something far more precious than silver ore.

The Colorado Kid had a beautiful friend he had to bury.